ADVENTURES
OF THE
No. 1 CAR SPOTTER

Other books by Atinuke

Too Small Tola
Too Small Tola and the Three Fine Girls
Too Small Tola Gets Tough
Too Small Tola Makes It Count

Anna Hibiscus
Hooray for Anna Hibiscus!
Good Luck, Anna Hibiscus!
Have Fun, Anna Hibiscus!
Welcome Home, Anna Hibiscus!
Go Well, Anna Hibiscus!
Love from Anna Hibiscus!
You're Amazing, Anna Hibiscus!

The No. 1 Car Spotter
The No. 1 Car Spotter and the Firebird
The No. 1 Car Spotter and the Car Thieves
The No. 1 Car Spotter Goes to School
The No. 1 Car Spotter and the Broken Road
The No. 1 Car Spotter Fights the Factory

For younger readers
Anna Hibiscus' Song
Splash, Anna Hibiscus!
Double Trouble for Anna Hibiscus!
Baby Goes to Market
B Is for Baby
Baby, Sleepy Baby
Catch That Chicken!
Hugo

Non-fiction
Africa, Amazing Africa: Country by Country

ADVENTURES OF THE No. 1 CAR SPOTTER

Atinuke

illustrated by Warwick Johnson Cadwell

This is a work of fiction. Names, characters, places and incidents are either the product of the author's imagination or, if real, used fictitiously. All statements, activities, stunts, descriptions, information and material of any other kind contained herein are included for entertainment purposes only and should not be relied on for accuracy or replicated as they may result in injury.

First published individually as *The No. 1 Car Spotter* (2010),
The No. 1 Car Spotter and the Firebird (2011)
and *The No. 1 Car Spotter and the Car Thieves* (2012)
by Walker Books Ltd 87 Vauxhall Walk, London SE11 5HJ

This edition published 2025

2 4 6 8 10 9 7 5 3 1

Text © 2010, 2011, 2012 by Atinuke
Illustrations © 2010, 2011, 2012 by Warwick Johnson Cadwell

The right of Atinuke and Warwick Johnson Cadwell to be identified as author and illustrator respectively of this work has been asserted in accordance with the Copyright, Designs and Patents Act 1988

EU Authorized Representative: HackettFlynn Ltd, 36 Cloch Choirneal, Balrothery, Co. Dublin, K32 C942, Ireland. EU@walkerpublishinggroup.com

This book has been typeset in Stempel Schneidler and Lauren

Printed and bound by CPI Group (UK) Ltd, Croydon CR0 4YY

All rights reserved. No part of this book may be reproduced, transmitted, or stored in an information retrieval system in any form or by any means, graphic, electronic, or mechanical, including photocopying, taping, and recording, without prior written permission from the publisher. Additionally, no part of this book may be used or reproduced in any manner for the purpose of training artificial intelligence technologies or systems, nor for text and data mining.

British Library Cataloguing in Publication Data:
a catalogue record for this book is available from the British Library

ISBN 978-1-5295-2690-5

www.walker.co.uk

Contents

The No. 1 Car Spotter	7
The No. 1 Car Spotter	11
No. 1 Goes to Market	43
7UP	71
No. 1 and the Wheelbarrow	93
The No. 1 Car Spotter and the Firebird	117
No. 1 and the Catapult	121
No. 1 and the Flood	145
Mama Coca-Cola's New House	169
The No. 1 Chop-House	189
The No. 1 Car Spotter and the Car Thieves	211
The No. 1 Car Spotter in the Palm Tree	215
No. 1 Opens His Big Mouth	241
The No. 1 Car Spotter Is Stolen	259
The No. 1 Car Spotter Spots the Car Thieves	279

THE Nº 1 CAR SPOTTER

by Atinuke

illustrated by Warwick Johnson Cadwell

WALKER
BOOKS

For my brother Ben
Writer, Adventurer and Car Spotter
A.

To my gang, D, S, H and W
W.JC.

The No. 1 Car Spotter

On the continent of Africa, you will find my country, Nigeria. In Nigeria there are many cities, all with skyscrapers, hotels, offices. There are also many smaller towns, all with tap water and electricity and television. Then there is my village, where we only talk about such things.

My village has a few compounds and many goats and several cows. It is in between the forest and the river and the road. The main road. The road brings cars past our village; many cars speeding towards the cities and the towns.

There are some few people in our village.

My best friend, Coca-Cola, lives in one compound with his old grandmother, his newborn sisters, Sunshine and Smile, and his mother, Mama Coca-Cola.

My sister's best friend, Nike, lives in another compound with her two elder brothers, Emergency and Tuesday, and her father, Uncle Go-Easy.

Beke, Bisi and Bola, the small children, live with their mother, Mama B, and Auntie Fine-Fine.

There are other people, in other compounds, but these are the people who know me well.

I live in a compound with my grandfather (who taught me everything I know), with my grandmother (who wants me to obey everything *she* knows), with my sister, Sissy, (who thinks I know nothing) and with my mother, who loves and feeds and looks after us all. My father, of course, lives in the city.

Let me introduce myself. My name is Oluwalase Babatunde Benson. But everybody calls me No. 1. The No. 1.

I am the No. 1 car spotter in my village. Car spotting is the only hobby in this village. Grandmother, Mama and all the aunties think that no such hobby should be allowed.

"Spotting cars does not take the goats to grass," Grandmother complains.

"It does not water the cows," Mama insists.

"Cars do not collect firewood," Auntie Fine-Fine confuses.

"Or carry yams from the fields," Mama Coca-Cola agrees.

"Cars won't fill your belly," Sissy joins in.

Sissy thinks spotting cars should be banned by the government. Sissy thinks that because I spot cars I am not doing my share of the work. But it is not true. I work hard all day. I do everything Mama and Grandmother and Coca-Cola's mother and my Auntie Fine-Fine and Uncle Go-Easy and everybody else in the village tell me to do. But while I am doing it I spot cars!

Who can help spotting cars when the road runs directly past the village? It is what we men do.

Grandfather, sitting under the iroko tree in the centre of the village, shouts, "Firebird!"

Uncle Go-Easy, waist-deep in the river, pulling in his nets, shouts, "Peugeot 505!"

Tuesday and Emergency, clearing the bush for a new field, hear an engine and shout, "Mercedes 914!"

Coca-Cola and I, high in the palm trees collecting nuts, shout, "Aston Martin DB5!"

Our village might be a poor village, lost in the bush, but a No. 1 road goes directly past it.

And I am the No. 1 car spotter! I can spot cars before I see them. From the sound of their engines, running sweet or backfiring, I know them.

"Daewoo! Suzuki! Land Cruiser!"

It was Grandfather who taught me to be a car spotter. He spends his old age under the iroko tree watching the road. When I was a baby I stayed with him there in the shade of the tree while Mama worked on our farm. Grandfather taught me my ABC. My 123.

"Peugeot, Passat, Porsche…!"

What Grandfather does not know about spotting cars is not to know.

Grandfather and I love all cars. But I love the Corolla the best. It is the No. 1-and-only car of our village!

One time when I was very small I heard its engine from far. Grandfather told me what it was.

"Toyota Corolla," he said.

He held me up on my small legs to see. I saw dust. I saw smoke. I saw the Toyota Corolla crawl into the village. I saw it cut out right in front of me. I saw the driver wave down a taxi to return to the city with his head in his hands.

Since then the Corolla has been there in the heart of the village. Every time my cousin Wale the mechanic comes from the town he looks at it and shakes his head. It will not go. It will never carry us around like rich people. But it is still my favourite car. Often I dream I am driving this car along the road, fast!

"No. 1, what are you dreaming about! Go and carry the yams from the field!" shouted Mama suddenly.

"Pick mango and orange! Ripe and sweet!" called Grandmother.

"Bring my beans!" commanded Mama Coca-Cola.

"The palm oil! The palm oil!" Auntie Fine-Fine joined in.

I started to run in all directions at once. Coca-Cola and Sissy and Emergency and Tuesday and Nike joined me.

Even Beke, Bisi and Bola started carrying baskets higher than themselves from the storeroom! All of our mothers and aunties and grandmothers were shouting at once.

The next day was market day. We would sell our palm oil and our yams, our onions, our tomatoes and our chilli peppers, our baskets and our dried fish, our oranges, mangos, rice...

With the money we would buy the important things we needed that only money can buy. Salt, sugar, kerosene for lamps, pencils and shoes for school. Sweets. Those things we cannot grow in our fields. Or pick from the trees of the forest. Or hunt in the bush. Or fish from the river.

I was running back with a basket of ripe mangos on my head when I heard a sharp crack.

Grandmother screamed and all the aunties started crying. Emergency and Tuesday had been pulling the old wooden cart into position, ready to load with all our goods for market.

"Then we heard a crack!" wailed Mama B.

"Like a gun firing," moaned Mama Coca-Cola.

"But it was the cart don' die-o!" Mama cried.

"Only God can save us now!" wept Auntie Fine-Fine.

They were gathered around the cart, wringing their hands and tearing at their clothes. Coca-Cola and Sissy and Nike and I pushed in to see.

The cart had broken! Snapped in half!

"How will I sell my palm oil?" wailed Auntie Fine-Fine.

"How will I sell my yams?" wailed Mama.

"How will I sell my oranges and mangos?" wailed Grandmother.

"No pencils for school," Sissy sobbed.

"No sweets." Coca-Cola and I looked at each other.

"This cart must be fixed!" shouted Mama B.

Coca-Cola and I ran to help Grandfather up from under the iroko tree. Grandfather used to be a carpenter. The village carpenter. He walked stiffly around the cart. Then he shook his head.

"This one will never go again!" he said.

"You see!" shouted Grandmother. "This is where car spotting has got you! You are now a useless old man."

Grandfather shook his stick at her. "In the days when this village was full of men we would have cut a tree, planed the wood and fixed the cart. It is the village that has become useless. Not the man!" he shouted.

Grandmother sighed. She knew it was true. All of the men of the village (except for Grandfather and Uncle Go-Easy) now lived in the city, trying to find jobs and earn money to pay for shoes and medicine and schooling for us, their families. My father was there. Coca-Cola's father was there. Even some of the women were there.

"Before-before our village was so full of women," Mama sighed, "we could have carried everything to market on our heads."

"Now everybody loves to live in the city," wailed Mama Coca-Cola.

"And we are left with a broken old cart!" said Grandmother, sucking her teeth. "And a broken old man."

"And how will we get to market and back?" cried Sissy.

Grandfather sadly shook his head. He sat down on the back of the Corolla to rest his old-old legs.

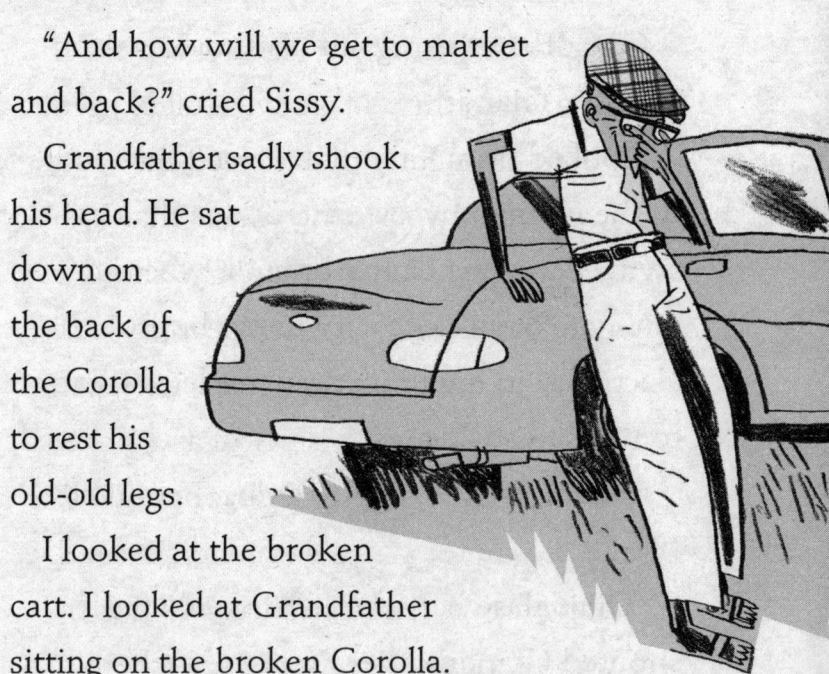

I looked at the broken cart. I looked at Grandfather sitting on the broken Corolla.

"Can't you make that machine work?" demanded Grandmother unreasonably, pointing to the Corolla. "You who love cars so much?"

Grandfather shook his head once again. "This one," he said, patting the Corolla, "will never go again."

"Is that all you can say!" shouted the women.

Grandfather shrugged his shoulders and raised his hands.

I looked from Grandfather on the Corolla to the women by the cart. Suddenly a light switched on inside my brain. I, who did not even have electricity in my house! The electricity in my brain fired my legs. I started to run.

"No. 1! Where are you going?" shouted Mama.

"Oluwalase Babatunde Benson! Stop!" shouted Grandmother. "Come here!"

"Wait for me!" shouted Coca-Cola.

But I did not stop. I could not wait. The current was running and there was no OFF switch. I did not stop at the river. I did not stop at the farm. I ran all the way through the bush to the town and it took me from morning until night was about to fall.

I zigzagged through the houses until I saw my cousin's corrugated iron shop. The ground all around was littered with rags and scraps of metal and black with the oil that cars like to drink.

"Wale! Wale! Wale!" I banged on the door.
"Come back tomorrow!" his voice replied.
"Is me! No. 1!" I shouted.
The door opened.
"Ah-ah! Oluwalase Babatunde Benson!" my cousin exclaimed. "Small brother!" He acknowledged that indeed we had the same grandmother and the same grandfather. "Way-tin?" He wanted to know what I was doing here in town all alone, banging on his door in the night.

I told him my idea. I told him everything.

"Slow down, slow down," he said at first. And then he said, *"Na-wa-oh!"* which means Wow!

He called his friends and drew my idea in the dirt for them to look at. I was just a small boy compared to them. But I had a big idea.

They nodded their heads, collected their equipment and together we ran back to the village.

When we arrived it was deep night. Grandmother and Mama were waiting for me, crying.

"Do you want to kill me!" Mama shouted.

"Do you not know that crocodiles and leopards and towns can eat a small boy like you!" Grandmother shouted.

"Lazy boy!" shouted Sissy from the house. She had to do my work that day.

But I did not stop to defend myself. I kept running until we reached the Corolla. We off-loaded the equipment and set to work right away. There was no time for palava. No time for wahala. No time for all this shouting. Tomorrow was market day!

The whole village woke when metal started grinding against metal. All the people gathered around the red sparks flying from the screaming Corolla. Only Coca-Cola's old grandmother stayed sleeping on her mat.

Grandfather came to stand beside me. He put his hand on my shoulder.

"*Ku ise, o, eyin omo mi*. Good work," he said to Wale and his friends.

"*A dupe, o,* Grandfather," they replied. "Thank you."

When the stars began to fade, metal kissed red metal together. Dawn was bright in the sky. The machines were silent. The mechanics were still.

Grandmother opened her mouth.

"Shh!" said Grandfather.

I left the chopped-up Corolla. I brought all the cows to the village and hitched them all up to our new Corolla-cart!

"Na-wa-oh!" gasped my mother.
"Na-wa-oh!" shouted my grandmother.
"Na-wa-oh!" whispered my sister.
"Sorry-o!" they all said, again and again. "Sorry."
Mama Coca-Cola and Auntie Fine-Fine were screaming with joy.
Uncle Go-Easy was walking around and around our new cart, shaking his head with wonder.
I led the cows around the village. It worked perfectly.
Wale and his friends whooped and shouted and jumped into one another's arms. They had won the World Cup for car cutting.

Grandfather shook their hands. Then he shook my hand. "Congratulations," he said.

"The fruit does not fall far from the tree," said Mama.

Grandfather and I smiled at each other. It was inside my head that the light switch had come on. But it was Grandfather who had done the wiring.

Then Grandfather shouted, "Where are the yams and the onions and the peppers and the mangos and the oranges and the dried fish and the rice and the palm oil? Is this village not going to market today?"

I laughed to see Mama and the aunties and the grandmothers all jump up and start to run around in every direction.

The No. 1 car spotter. That's me! Getting our village to market and back … in our new No. 1 Toyota Cow-rolla!

No.1 Goes to Market

Come on, you remember me! Oluwalase Babatunde? I am the No. 1 car spotter. The No. 1 car spotter in my village. Maybe the No. 1 car spotter in the world.

    Look at us now, the No. 1 village, escorting our new Toyota Cow-rolla into market!

We had loaded it with baskets piled high with yams, onions, tomatoes, plantains, chilli peppers, mangos, oranges, dried fish, rice, palm oil.

"This cart is strong-o!" crowed Mama.

"This one won't break-o!" agreed Grandmother.

"This cart could carry rock and stone!" said Mama B proudly.

We sang praise songs to the cart all the way to market and when the market people saw us arrive with our No. 1 vehicle you should have heard them shout!

"Wha' is dis? Can you believe it?"

"Ah-ah! Check out village pick-up!"

"Na new off-road style!"

Every man, woman and child ran to see how our ordinary village cows could be pulling one wonda-full imported Corolla.

Mama and the aunties got busy off-loading our goods but us men got busy telling everybody wha' happen.

"My boy, he achieve electricity for brain!" Grandfather boasted.

"The mechanic boys were sparking all night!" Uncle Go-Easy joined in from his dried fish stall.

"Sha! It was easy!" Wale crowed.

And then all the women stopped listening to us because Mama and the aunties had finished off-loading and suddenly we were surrounded by fat red tomatoes, bumpy biting chilli peppers, rice fresh on stalk, pungent dried fish, golden palm oil. The best in the market! And the women had come to market to buy. Then Mama Coca-Cola started frying akara and the men pushed to buy first.

Grandfather went to sleep in the cart. Wale disappeared with his friends. But I was kept busy helping Mama and the aunties and Uncle Go-Easy to sell.

"Bag – you need a bag?" Mama questioned a customer. "Bring a bag for this lady! Bring a bag for this lady!"

"Change!" bellowed Mama Coca-Cola. "I need small change!"

"Fresh water!" coughed Mama B.

"Thief!" screamed Grandmother. "Catch that boy! Reclaim my mango!"

I was busy running back and forth, back and forth in the heat, but I did not complain, not for one second. Nor did Sissy and Nike and Coca-Cola and Emergency and Tuesday. The more tomatoes and fish and oil we sold, the more pencils and sugar and flip-flops our mothers would buy for us. So we were like Olympic runners, quick off the mark. And if we jumped the gun, nobody complained.

When the sun was high in the sky the customers started to dry up. The baskets were low. The best of everything had gone. Mama and the aunties did not need our help any more.

But I saw Auntie Fine-Fine beckon to Sissy. She whispered into Sissy's ear and Sissy started to smile. Sissy's smile grew so big I wanted to know what stretched it out so wide.

I could read Auntie Fine-Fine's lips. "How much? Ask how much."

When Sissy ran off into the market I beckoned to Coca-Cola. We followed Sissy past the plantain sellers and the plastic cup traders, past the goats and the chickens and the plastic shoe traders and the mountains of yard cloth.

Suddenly Sissy stopped by a little stall loaded with small-small bottles and jars. The jars and bottles were all different colours of red and pink. The stall was surrounded by ladies young and old.

I braked behind a mountain of wax cloth. Coca-Cola crashed into me and we narrowly avoided toppling the new cloth into the dirt. Coca-Cola gave me a dirty look.

"No brake light! No indicator!" he

hissed at me. "I will book you!"

"Sorry, officer, sorry. I beg you!" I tried not to laugh.

Sissy turned round and looked. She shouted, "Don' think I don' see you there, No. 1! Did anybody send you here? I don't think so. Jus' wait till I tell Mama!"

The ladies at the stalls heard Sissy's words. They all turned around to stare at me. My face became hot. I turned and ran back. Coca-Cola overtook me. He hid behind the Cow-rolla.

Grandmother looked at me with narrowed eyes. Quickly I looked down at the ground. It was littered with squashed tomatoes and sweet wrappers. I grabbed Mama's broom and started to sweep. Grandmother smiled.

I was just about to load the empty baskets onto the cart and take the opportunity to court marshal Coca-Cola for deserting me under enemy fire when Sissy arrived back, empty-handed.

I busied myself sweeping. Sissy looked at me and opened her mouth loud. But before she could speak, Auntie Fine-Fine beckoned to her. "Price? Price?" I saw her ask.

Sissy bent and whispered in her ear, then straightened to look at me. As she opened her mouth again Mama B called, "Where have you been, Sissy? I want you and Nike

to take Beke and Bisi and Bola to buy plastic shoe. Good quality and cheap. Go now while there is still time!"

Sissy's mouth was still open. She was looking at me. But Mama shut her mouth for her by saying, "Did you not hear your auntie? What are you waiting for? Go!"

So Sissy and Nike went off into the market, holding onto Beke and Bisi and Bola.

I put down my brush and heaved a sigh of relief.

Auntie Fine-Fine called after Sissy but Sissy was gone. And shopping with Beke and Bisi and Bola would take a LONG time. You did not need a brain to know that. Auntie Fine-Fine looked around despondent and caught me looking at her. She smiled.

"No. 1!" she called.

I tried to hide behind my broom.

"No. 1!" Auntie Fine-Fine called again.

I saw Mama look at me when I did not answer.

"Yes, Auntie," I answered.

"Come here, good boy!" Auntie Fine-Fine called. "I want you to do something for me."

Mama narrowed her eyes at me, waiting for me to answer. What can a boy my size do in such a situation?

"Yes, Auntie!" I said again and went to Auntie Fine-Fine.

"Do you know the stall that sells many small-small bottles and containers?" she asked.

"Yes, Auntie," I replied. I looked around desperately for Coca-Cola. His legs were disappearing into the Cow-rolla. They were going nowhere with me.

"I want you to go there and buy me…" Auntie Fine-Fine gestured for me to come closer.

Grandmother looked up.

"*Lipstick,*" Auntie Fine-Fine whispered and pressed money in my hand.

Grandmother's eyes widened.

"Go!" Auntie Fine-Fine said.

I looked at Mama. She had not heard Auntie Fine-Fine say lipstick. Her eyes said obedience *or else*.

So I went. Past the plantains and plastic cups and the chickens and the goats and plastic shoes, where Sissy stared at me and sucked her teeth. When I got to the cloth stall again I stopped and hid.

I prayed that the stall I was headed for had gone. Lipstick was women's business. And women's business was not for a small boy like me. I did not want those ladies to laugh at me again.

But there the stall was, with all its small-small bottles and jars, and this time even more ... girls.

I was ready to wait behind the cloth until all the girls were gone when a big man pushed me out into the open.

"Can' you let a man pass!" he shouted.

All the girls turned around. But I opened my shoulders and made myself stand tall. I was the No. 1. What was I afraid of?

I pushed my way to the front of the stall as if it was nothing to me to be there. I stared at the bottles and jars. Which one was *lipstick*?

The trader leaned over the jars and looked at me.

"Wha' is a small boy like you doing here?" he said. "This is not where you will find football match or computer game!"

The girls started to giggle. Quickly I picked up one of the glass jars as if I knew what I was doing. I pushed Auntie Fine-Fine's money into the trader's hand. Then I ran away.

I ran all the way back and gave the jar to Auntie Fine-Fine. I started to join Coca-Cola in the Cow-rolla.

But before I had the chance to walk two steps Auntie Fine-Fine cried out, "What is this *thing*? This is not what I asked you to buy! What am I supposed to do with this? WHERE IS MY MONEY?"

All the women turned to look at me. It was too late to run.

"No. 1!" shouted Mama. "What have you done?"

"Nothing, Mama," I answered. "I do not know."

"What kin' answer is that?" my mother demanded.

I could see plenty of trouble coming and no sweets after all my hard work.

Mama stood up. Grandfather woke up to see what all the commotion was about. Coca-Cola's feet were trembling on my behalf. Auntie Fine-Fine was still shouting. Everybody was looking at me.

Suddenly Grandmother said, "Don' blame the boy. This woman sent him to buy lipstick! How should he know how to buy lipstick?"

There was a sudden silence as Grandmother's words were absorbed. Then all the aunties started to laugh. Mama laughed the loudest and patted my shoulders.

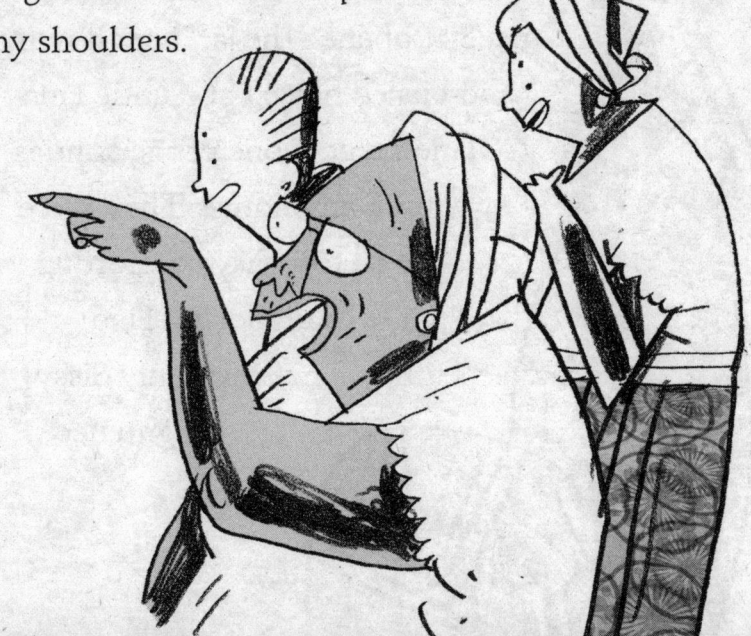

Auntie Fine-Fine stopped shouting and started to cry. The laughing aunties gathered around to comfort her. Auntie Fine-Fine's mouth was open so wide there was no room in her face for her eyes.

"My money-o! This useless thing for all my money-o!" she kept crying.

Sissy arrived back just then, dragging Beke, Bisi and Bola. She looked at me. She looked at Auntie Fine-Fine. She looked at the jar in Auntie Fine-Fine's hand.

Sissy took the jar. She winked at me. She opened the jar, bent down and busied herself at Auntie Fine-Fine's feet. None of the aunties took any notice. They were all too busy comforting Auntie Fine-Fine.

Suddenly Sissy straightened.

The aunties shrieked. Grandmother fell from her stool. Coca-Cola's head appeared over the top of the Cow-rolla cart. Grandfather shouted, *"What?"* We all stared at Auntie Fine-Fine's feet.

Auntie Fine-Fine closed her mouth in order to see what was going on. She looked at our bulging eyes. She looked down to see what we were ogling. Her toenails! They were *pink*. Bright hibiscus *pink*.

Auntie Fine-Fine did not move for almost one minute. Then slowly she smiled. She laughed. She clapped her hands. She rose to her feet and started to admire herself. All the other aunties commenced laughing and clapping too.

Auntie Fine-Fine started to dance right there in the market!

Then Auntie Fine-Fine came towards me. Grandfather gripped my shoulder.

"*Cleva boy!*" Auntie Fine-Fine shouted.

"Go buy me one!" Mama B demanded.

"Red one! I want a red one!" yelled Mama Coca-Cola.

"*Cleva boy!*" Auntie Fine-Fine repeated, squeezing my cheek.

She pressed some money in my hand. It was enough to buy sweets *and* puff-puff doughnuts! I smiled my No. 1 smile.

Now all the aunties were pressing money on me. "Go and buy! Go and buy!" they shouted.

Mama was laughing. Grandmother shaking her head. Trouble was still shaking me with its teeth! But Sissy took pity on me. She took the aunties' money and ran back to that stall.

It was time to go. We were tired. We were happy to load our salt and sugar and kerosene and cloth into the Cow-rolla and ride home. Speaking for myself, my stomach was so full of puff-puff and sweets I could not have walked.

But not Auntie Fine-Fine. Auntie Fine-Fine insisted on walking. "I can see my feet better like this," she said.

I looked down at Auntie Fine-Fine's feet flashing in the road.

"Porsche," I said. Coca-Cola looked up and down the road.

"Where?" He asked.

I nodded down at Auntie Fine-Fine's toes flashing in the dirt. Coca-Cola and I laughed. Ten pink Porsche convertibles were stirring up the dust!

7UP

Greetings from the No. 1. The No. 1 car spotter in my village, maybe the No. 1 car spotter in the whole world!

One time I came close to losing my name. Only one time. It happen like this. When I am not with Grandfather under the iroko trees spotting cars, I am with Coca-Cola. Coca-Cola is my tight friend. He has the coolest name in the village.

Coca-Cola got his own name because his mother, Mama Coca-Cola, sells akara by the roadside. She fries exactly the right blend of beans and onions and chilli peppers and salt to hit a person's pocket. The smell travels straight from the person's nose direct to the person's belly, from there it goes direct to the person's cash, which lands immediately in Mama Coca-Cola's hand. And the akara tastes so good that once you have eaten one you have to eat more. And once you have eaten more you need to take something to make room for even more. And nothing washes akara down better (Mama Coca-Cola knows) than cold soft drinks.

So Mama Coca-Cola stores her soft drinks in the river in order to serve them chilled. It is Coca-Cola's job to carry the Coca-Cola, Fanta, 7UP and Sprite from the river to the customer. And Mama Coca-Cola's shorthand way of telling him that customers are waiting for drinks is to shout, "Coca-Cola!" at the top of her voice.

Once upon a time Coca-Cola had a traditional name but now everybody just calls him Coca-Cola.

One day I was with Coca-Cola in his compound when it was time for him to eat. Of course Mama Coca-Cola called me to eat also. Akara is not the only food Mama Coca-Cola knows how to cook well. I ate and ate and ate; in the end my belly weighed so much I could not carry myself back to my own compound to sleep. When Coca-Cola lay down for the night I collapsed next to him.

In the morning as soon as I woke up
I knew that I was in Mama Coca-Cola's
house. Instead of being surrounded by
the noises of my family already at work,
sweeping the compound and washing
clothes, I was surrounded by snores.
Coca-Cola's family loves to
sleep. Maybe it is because
of the mountain of food
they consume on a nightly
basis. A full belly loves
to sleep, it has no need to
complain, no need to wake.
The rest of the village wakes early. Before
the first cock-crow, before the first light. And
every morning, when we are already hard
at work, we always hear Mama Coca-Cola
wake with a shout. Then we see her run
down to her stall, still tying her wrappa, to
begin frying akara with Sunshine and Smile
still at her breast and the first bus already past!

This morning they were still snoring when I awoke. It was dark but I sat up immediately. Grandmother would be needing me to collect firewood. Mama would be calling me to hoe the fields. Sissy would need my help with the goats. My sitting up woke Sunshine and Smile. They opened their baby eyes, and started to laugh, then to cry for food. Mama Coca-Cola opened her eyes. She looked to the window to see how much of the morning had already passed.

When she saw that the sun had not even reached the sky, that only the cockerels crowing and the sounds of the village awakening were indications of its impending arrival, Mama Coca-Cola was so happy. She

jumped to her feet, squeezed my cheeks, and started shouting, "Onions! Beans! Frying pan! Stool!"

Coca-Cola shot off his mat and started to run around. As I was an able-bodied boy in the vicinity of a shouting mama I started to run around as well. By the time we had collected everything Mama Coca-Cola had fed Sunshine and Smile and adjusted her wrappa. She was ready to go down to her position on the road. Before the village knew what was happening the smell of frying akara had filled the air and those who had not yet eaten found their bellies propelling their legs towards last night's leftovers.

The first bus arrived. "Coca-Cola!"

Coca-Cola and I started to run. We laughed as we ran to the river. Happily I loaded my arms with cold bottles. Running for Mama Coca-Cola meant akara. For breakfast, lunch and dinner.

I was licking my fingers when the second bus arrived.

"Coca-Cola! 7UP!" Mama Coca-Cola shouted.

I was happy to run back to the river. I would run anywhere for Mama Coca-Cola's akara.

On my way I passed Sissy, my sister, taking our goats to graze in the hot, dusty, dry bush.

"No. 1!" she shouted. "Come here and take the goats to grass!"

"I am answering Mama Coca-Cola!" I shouted back.

Sissy sucked her teeth. "Greedy boy!" she shouted.

I ignored her.

I was just licking my fingers when three BMWs stopped in front of Mama Coca-Cola's stall. We did not wait for her to shout. Coca-Cola and I started running to the river. I passed Grandmother.

"No. 1! Firewood!" she shouted.

I shouted back again, "I answer Mama Coca-Cola!"

Grandmother shook her broom at me. "Just le' me catch you!" she shouted. But I knew she couldn't.

On the way back we passed the iroko tree. Emergency was sitting there with Grandfather.

"Mammy wagon!" Emergency shouted.

I looked at the road. There was the mammy wagon approaching, rocking from side to side with many, many passengers. I off-loaded my bottles into Coca-Cola's arms and turned around to run back to the river for more.

"You are allowing your stomach to rule your legs!" Grandfather said on my way back.

I pretended I did not hear him.

The following morning I woke once again in Mama Coca-Cola's house. The previous evening I had allowed her to reward my hard work with another mountain of delicious food.

Once again I sat up in the dark. Sunshine and Smile started to clamour for food. Mama Coca-Cola opened her eyes and smiled.

By the time the first bus arrived, the akara was ready.

"Coca-Cola! 7UP!" Mama Coca-Cola shouted.

Fresh akara had fuelled my engine. My legs were pistons carrying me down to the river.

On the way I passed

Mama. She was going to wash our clothes in the river.

"Good morning, Coca-Cola! Good morning, 7UP!" she said.

My engine stuttered.

I passed Sissy and Nike, their heads loaded with firewood.

"Look, it's the soft drinks!" said Sissy.

"Good morning, Coca-Cola! Good morning, 7UP!" Nike giggled.

My engine faltered.

On the way back from the river we saw Uncle Go-Easy. "You boys! Coca-Cola! 7UP!" he shouted.

"Make sure you no touch my fishing net when you go for river!"

I braked immediately.

"Stop!" I shouted to Coca-Cola.

I loaded all my soft drinks on top of his.

"Wha' happen?" he asked.

"Tell your mother that Grandmother is waiting for me to sweep the yard, I have to escort our goats to the bush, and Sissy and Mama are waiting for me ... to take care of ... everything!"

"Don' you wan' to help me?" Coca-Cola asked. "Are you tired of akara already?"

I did not answer. I ran into our compound.

"So!" Grandmother said. "Did your belly tire of superior food?"

"Yes! No, Grandmother," I replied looking meekly at the ground.

"What are you waiting for?" she snapped. "Sweep the compound! Take the cows to drink at the river! Take the goats to the bush! Don't come back until you have collected firewood! Go!"

Down by the river with the cows, I met Coca-Cola, his arms loaded with soft drinks. He looked sadly at me.

"Why don' you help me?" he asked.

"Coca-Cola," I said, "I am the No. 1. THE No. 1. I am not 7UP."

"But why?" said Coca-Cola. "W'a's wrong with 7UP?"

"Because," I said, "No. 1 is number ONE. Who wants to be called 7UP when he can be called NUMBER ONE? No. 1 is first in line. Seven has to wait until one, two, three, four, five and six have all passed before you reach him."

Coca-Cola said nothing. He looked at the river. Then he said, "I am Coca-Cola."

"That," I said, "is because Coca-Cola is the number one soft drink. Some people prefer Fanta. It is true. And some people prefer Sprite. Some people don't touch Coca-Cola. But Coca-Cola is still the number one."

And before either of us could say anything more we heard Mama Coca-Cola shouting, "Coca-Cola! Coca-Cola! Where is that boy?"

Coca-Cola ran back. I walked slowly back from the river with the cows. I passed the iroko tree. Grandfather was there. I stopped. Grandfather said nothing. He was watching the road. Suddenly my mouth opened.

"Coca-Cola is my tight friend," I said.

"I have noticed," said Grandfather.

"Now he is running back and forth, back and forth," I said as Coca-Cola ran past.

"Every two seconds," Grandfather said.

"I will help him." I said. "No. 7 is not so far behind No. 1."

"Your mother and grandmother and sister also need you—" Grandfather started to say.

"No. 1! No. 1!"

It was Auntie Fine-Fine.

"Your mother said I should call you," she said. "The palm nuts are ripe!"

Grandfather looked at me. He raised his eyebrows.

So I quickly returned the cows to the compound and turned towards the farm. Palm nuts give palm oil. Soup and stew are made with palm oil. Yam and plantain are fried in palm oil. Where there is nothing else we dip our soft food in palm oil. In fact, without palm oil, there is no such thing as good food.

As soon as I reached the farm, I attached my rope around my waist and started to climb.

I smiled. Who cannot be happy up in a tree?

(At least in the first hour, before the back and legs begin to ache!)

From the ground Mama and the aunties were shouting, "Make you hurry-o!"

"Let me not stand here all day waiting to collect!"

"Don' forget before you eat the oil, we have to press the nut!"

"Reach the top! Why go-slow?"

I pretend I cannot hear them. From high in the tree I can see the whole village, the whole road. There is Grandfather under the iroko tree. There is Grandmother supervising the children of the village and readying herself to press palm oil. And there is Coca-Cola and Mama Coca-Cola by the road, waiting for customers.

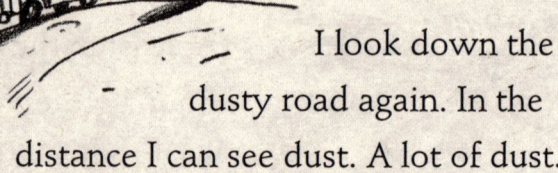

I look down the dusty road again. In the distance I can see dust. A lot of dust.

I lean out of my tree in the direction of Mama Coca-Cola's stall.

"BUS!" I scream. "Bus come soon!"

Coca-Cola leaps up. He looks down the road. He can see nothing. Mama Coca-Cola shakes her head.

"BUS!" I scream again.

Again Coca-Cola leaps up. And this time they recognize my voice. And they remember that I am the No. 1. The No. 1 car spotter in the village.

Mama Coca-Cola starts to cook akara double time.

Coca-Cola runs fast to the river and carries many bottles back to the stall. He has time to make two journeys.

By this time the bus is announcing itself with its growling engine.

From where I am
   in the tree, I can see the bus stop
and passengers alight. I can see the bottles
of cold soft drinks dripping on the table. I
can see people digging in their wallets.

By the end of the day I have cut many
bunches of palm nuts, all of which Mama
and Grandmother are just now squeezing
into fresh, orange-red, tasty palm oil which
they will use to cook our food.

I have also alerted Mama Coca-Cola
to the imminent arrival of twenty-three
vehicles.

That night I am happy to be in my own compound with Mama and Grandmother and Grandfather and Sissy.

Outside the compound I can hear Mama Coca-Cola talking loudly to everybody.

"My stall is now the No. 1 stall. The No. 1 stall on the road. And it is because of that boy."

I catch Coca-Cola's eye peeping through the gateway. He smiles.

"That boy," I hear Mama Coca-Cola say to the whole village, "is truly the No. 1! The No. 1 car spotter on the road!"

No. 1 and the Wheelbarrow

It's me! The No. 1 car spotter! Spotting cars from the No. 1 spot under the iroko tree.

This is where Grandfather sits. Grandfather, the No. 1 of all the No. 1s.

"It used to be that there was only one car on the road," Grandfather remembers. "The Peugeot—"

"403!" I shout. "Followed by 404."

"But now things are much more interesting," says Grandfather. "There are many more cars to spot, many more types to memorize, many more makes to identify.

"Take the Pontiac Firebird, for example," Grandfather sighs. "There is only one in the whole country. ONE. And it belongs to a university professor. This is no area-boy car. The Firebird! It used to pass by here any time Prof went to his village."

In the good old days Grandfather would challenge me. "Which one can you remember?"

"Aston Martin, Audi, Bentley, Cadillac, Citroën, Daewoo, Eclipse, Ferrari, Fiat, Ford, Golf, Honda, Isuzu, Jaguar, Jeep, Komatsu, Land Rover, Lamborghini, Lada, Mitsubishi, Nissan, Opel, Pontiac, Peugeot, Porsche, Rolls-Royce, Skoda, Saab, Toyota, Uno, Volvo, Vauxhall, VW, X-90, Yamaha, Zimmer…"

And Grandfather would nod his head. "Good. Good."

Those were the good old days.

Then came the bad.

Grandfather and I were still under the iroko tree. But in silence, alone. Grandfather had sent away all the people who sometimes sat with him there. We watched the road. But we were not spotting cars. Our thoughts were in Grandmother's room.

Grandmother was sick. She could not come out of her room. It was clear to everybody, Grandmother needed a medical doctor to perform a miracle. Or she would die.

Grandfather counted all his money. Every naira note and kobo coin he had saved over the years. His money was not enough for medical miracle.

Mama counted all her money. All the money my father had sent her that she had managed to save. It was not enough for medicine.

Not even together with Grandfather's money. The money did not reach.

My father worked hard in the city to provide us all with shoes and school and medicine. Money like that can only be earned in the city.

My mother sent a message to my father for money. Money to save Grandmother's life.

Mama sent the message through one taxi driver who often passed our village on his way to and from the city. The taxi driver knew my father. He knew where my father worked as a gardener in a rich man's compound in the city.

But when the taxi driver next passed he told us that he had not found my father there. The rich man had gone and so had all his people. And nobody knew what had happened to my father.

Since then Grandfather has not moved from the iroko tree. I have not moved from Grandfather. Grandmother cannot move from her bed. Mama does not move from Grandmother's room. And Sissy struggles alone with the goats and the cows and everything. She does not sing. She does not smile or laugh.

The aunties struggle on the farms with their babies on their backs and at their feet. Grandmother was no longer in the compound ready to look after them all. The aunties abandon their farms early in the day to bring us food.

"Eat! Eat!" they begged.

How could we eat? Grandmother was fading before our very eyes. And Papa had disappeared.

Suddenly Grandfather stood up. He looked down the road. I looked too. *What?* There was nothing.

Grandfather tried to walk towards the road. But in the time he had been sitting, sitting, sitting under the tree, his bones had become old and stiff. Grandfather fell down.

I shouted. Mama came from the house to see why. Sissy came to help me raise Grandfather from the ground.

When he was back on his feet Grandfather turned again towards the road, using my shoulder for a walking stick.

Then somebody came into view walking down the road. Grandfather forgot he was old. Grandfather tried to run.

Suddenly Grandfather was not alone in running. My legs and Sissy's legs were also possessed by joy. We overtook Grandfather.

"Papa! Papa! Papa!"

Mama came running out of Grandmother's room. "Akin! Akin! Akin!"

It was my father. Home! He took us all in his arms. He smelled of sweat and tiredness.

The whole village came to celebrate. They brought food for us again that night.

"You see," Auntie Fine-Fine whispered. "One problem has solved. The other will also solve."

"Now that he has returned, Old Mama will improve," agreed Uncle Go-Easy.

"He will look after everything," said Mama Coca-Cola. "You have no more need to worry."

On every face hope was shining. But not on Papa's face.

"Our son has returned!" I heard Grandfather whisper to Grandmother from the door of her room.

But when he thought everybody was asleep I head Papa say this: "My wife, I have no more job. Oga moved abroad one month ago. Since then I have been applicant. I have been going from one place to another. They all say the same thing. No job. No job. No job. *Olori mi*, I have no money for doctor."

My father cried.

The next day I did not sit with Grandfather. I could see him under the iroko tree. He kept looking towards my mother's room. He was waiting for my father to come out and call a taxi to carry Grandmother to the medical centre. He was wondering why his son did not come out quickly.

I hid behind Mama Coca-Cola's stall. Mama Coca-Cola looked at me. She looked up at Grandfather. She looked for a long time at our quiet compound.

Mama Coca-Cola sighed. She cooked fresh akara for me.

"Four-by-four!" Coca-Cola shouted.

I looked up. Four-by-four was Mike. The NGO. Non-Government Organization man. Call him what you like. He had come from the city to build the medical centre. And he had brought the palm nut press.

"Hi, Mike! Hi, Mike!" Coca-Cola was shouting "Hi!" city-style just like Mike had taught us. I did not even feel like smiling.

Mike bought all of us cold drinks. Me and Sissy and Coca-Cola and Nike and Bisi and Bola and Beke and Emergency and Tuesday and the others.

"How is Grandmother today?" Mike looked at me.

I shook my head.

Mike looked sad. "She needs to go to the medical centre," he said. "I can give her a lift there."

I shook my head. "No money for doctor," I said.

Mike looked sad. Then he smiled. "Hey, I have something for you," he said.

I looked at him. Mike never gave us money but sometimes he had chocolate. Sometimes he had chewing gum.

"Wheelbarrows!" said Mike. "Free to anybody who can sign. To improve village life."

Coca-Cola and I looked at each other.

"Come on," said Mike. "Surely smart kids like you can write your names?"

"I can do that!" I shouted.

Last time Cousin Overtime was here she had taught Sissy and Coca-Cola and me to write our names.

"Excellent!" said Mike. "This village could do with a few wheelbarrows!"

He took some papers from his four-by-four car and showed us where to sign.

"Wheelbarrows are to improve village life. They are not for selling," he told us again.

Sissy, Coca-Cola and I nodded. "Yes, Mike. OK, Mike."

We signed. Then Mike unloaded three wheelbarrows from the back of his four-by-four.

Mama Coca-Cola was dancing and singing and clapping around Coca-Cola's wheelbarrow. It would carry many soft drinks back and forth from the river.

Mike smiled, beeped his horn and drove away.

Sissy and I slowly pushed our wheelbarrows up towards our compound. Papa was sitting under the iroko tree with Grandfather, at last. They both looked as stiff as the tree.

"What is this?" Papa asked.

"It is an NGO wheelbarrow, Papa," I replied.

"To improve village life," said Sissy.

Papa jumped to his feet and started to shout, "Who will pay for this?"

"They were free, Papa!" Sissy was crying.

I could see Papa was struggling to believe her.

"The NGO gave them to us, Papa," I said. "We only had to sign."

Papa looked at Grandfather.

"He is the man who brought us the palm oil press," Grandfather said. "The same one who built the school and the medical centre. He is a good man."

For a long time Papa was silent. Then he said, "Will he come to take them back?"

"No, Papa," I said.

"And he does not expect us to pay later?" Papa asked.

"No, Papa," said Sissy, "they were free. To improve village life."

At last Papa nodded. He walked around the wheelbarrows. He looked at us.

"No. 1, Sissy," he said seriously, "I need those wheelbarrows."

"Take them, Papa," I said.

Sissy nodded.

Our father took the wheelbarrows. He loaded one into the other.

"You are good children," he said.

Without saying another word, without saying goodbye, Papa pushed the wheelbarrows down the road in the direction of the city. Grandfather and Sissy and I watched.

Papa ran.

Two days later, the taxi man came with an envelope for Mama. In that envelope was money from Papa. Enough money for Grandmother to go to the medical centre, and for a taxi too.

Mama shouted and cried. Mama Coca-Cola started to shout, "Taxi! Taxi!" even though the taxi man was already there.

Grandfather rose to his feet and started to praise God. Sissy started to cry. And all the aunties came to carry Grandmother gently and place her in the taxi next to Mama. We waved goodbye.

Grandfather and I watched the road for two days. On the third day Mama and Grandmother came back. Grandmother was on her own two feet. For the second time in one week Grandfather ran up the road. For the second time he was overtaken. But when at last he reached her, the person who held onto her the longest was Grandfather himself.

One month after that, the taxi man passed again. Again he stopped. This time he had a photograph for us.

A photograph of my father.

In the photograph Papa was standing with another man. They were both pushing wheelbarrows loaded high with sacks and bags and boxes.

"This is your father's new business," the taxi man explained. "He carries people's goods from one place to another. And this is his business partner."

We all looked closely at the photograph. On my father's face was a big smile.

I saw that on Sissy's face and Mama's face and Grandmother's face and Grandfather's face there was a big smile too. But not on mine.

Every time I heard a four-by-four I went down to the river to hide.

"What are you doing here?" asked Uncle Go-Easy. "Is that not your friend's four-by-four that I hear?"

I did not say anything.

"Do you not like choco-whatever any more?" Uncle Go-Easy persisted.

I did not say anything.

"The man give you wheelbarrows to save Grandmother's life and you don' like him any more?" Uncle Go-Easy was not giving up.

"He said the wheelbarrow was to improve village life!" I said, trying not to cry.

"And so?" Uncle Go-Easy did not understand.

"I signed," I said, "to improve village life."

"Is that so?" asked Uncle Go-Easy.

"And Papa took them to the city," I concluded, crying.

"Ahhh," Uncle Go-Easy nodded his head.

He took me gently by the arm and steered me back towards the village.

"Look!" he said, nodding towards our compound.

There were Beke and Bisi and Bola and Sunshine and Smile and all the other small babies playing with Grandmother.

Uncle Go-Easy cocked his ear towards the farms.

I could hear their mothers, the aunties, along with my mother, singing as they hoed their fields together without babies on their backs or under their feet.

"We will eat well next year!" they sang.

"Look!" Uncle Go-Easy pointed back down the path.

Sissy and her friend Nike were walking to

the river with buckets of washing. Laughing!

"Look again!" He pointed up to the iroko tree.

Underneath the tree Grandfather was sitting happily, chanting the Odu Ifa and waving his fly swat. People sat beside him, drinking in his words and nodding their heads.

Suddenly I understood! The two wheelbarrows in the city had made Grandmother well. Now Grandmother could look after the babies again and the aunties could work well in the fields. They meant that we would all eat well next year. In fact, two wheelbarrows in the city were a big improvement on village life!

I looked up at Uncle Go-Easy.

"Go easy, No. 1," he said, walking back to the river.

I watched him go. Then I heard the four-by-four engine even clearer. I looked up at the road. I could not see it clearly yet but I knew.

"Mike! Hi, Mike!" I shouted and ran towards the road.

As I passed I heard Grandfather shout, "You see that boy? He is the No. 1! The No. 1 car spotter in the world!"

THE Nº1 CAR SPOTTER

and the Firebird

by Atinuke

illustrated by Warwick Johnson Cadwell

Walker
BOOKS

For my father
A.

To my gang once again,
D, S, H and W
W.JC.

No. 1 and the Catapult

My name is Oluwalase Babatunde Benson. But everybody calls me No. 1. I am the No. 1 car spotter. The No. 1 car spotter in Nigeria.

My village is not like the towns and cities in Nigeria. We do not have television, or even electricity. We do not have shops, or even traffic lights.

We have our compounds, where we live. We have our farms, where we work. We have the river, where we play. And best of all we have the road that runs past the village, carrying buses and lorries and cars from one city to another.

And I am the No. 1 car spotter. I know the cars before I see them by the sound of their engines, sweet or back-firing. I call their names before they even appear.

That is why they call me No. 1!

I can spot one now!

"Firebird!" I shout.

The Firebird passes in a whirlwind of dust. It is a red speck leading the tornado.

I stop leading the cows to the river with my best friend, Coca-Cola, to watch. Uncle Go-Easy stops mending his nets to watch. His boys, Tuesday and Emergency, stop hoeing the fields to watch. Even Grandfather stops his fly whisk to watch.

All this stop-stopping of our work annoys the women, who have not stopped their work to watch.

"Why are the goats not in the bush?" Grandmother suddenly shouts.

"No. 1!" Mama calls. "You who are so quick to shout and so slow to work! O-ya!"

"Coca-Cola! Take the goats with No. 1!" shouts Coca-Cola's mother.

Coca-Cola and I both groan. We were going to swim in the cool river. Now we will have to trek into the hot-hot bush.

"That is where car spotting gets you," says my sister, Sissy. And she and her best friend, Nike, laugh.

We only have time to narrow our eyes at them before we run. Already all the women in the village are releasing their goats from their compounds. We must escort the goats to the bush where they look for food and we keep them from becoming lost.

The bush is hot. There is no shade. The air is like oil on the road. Suddenly something moves.

"Snake!" I shout.

Coca-Cola pulls out his catapult. *Ping!* The big snake reverses fast into the bush.

"You see that, No. 1!" Coca-Cola crows.

"Good one," I say. I don't say more. It is too hot anyway.

Coca-Cola hits a small rock. He hits a bush. He hits a leaf. My catapult does not leave my pocket. There is no point.

When we return to the village, Coca-Cola boasts. "I dispatched one big-big snake double-triple quick!"

"What about you, No. 1?" Sissy asks.

"I could have hit a leopard with one shot," I lie.

"No. 1!" Sissy laughs. "You could not hit an elephant!"

It is true. And everybody laughs at me. I scratch the ground with my foot. Sissy, Nike, Coca-Cola, Emergency and Tuesday take out their catapults to practise.

I look away. I see something.

"Firebird!" I shout.

On the road a tiny speeding something is growing bigger. Soon the something is clearly red. The Firebird zooms back past the village!

Sissy, Nike, Coca-Cola, Emergency and Tuesday are now talking about when they will be big hunters. How the village will sing their praise songs.

"Of course, you will all be big hunters," I join in. "You will eat meat every day. And when I pass you in my big car, listening to my big stereo on my way from one big city to another, I will honk my horn and wave to you."

I run to join Grandfather under the iroko tree before they laugh at me again.

Grandfather is always under the iroko tree. It is his place as an old man. To sit in the only shade in the village where he can observe everything and everybody without tiring his neck.

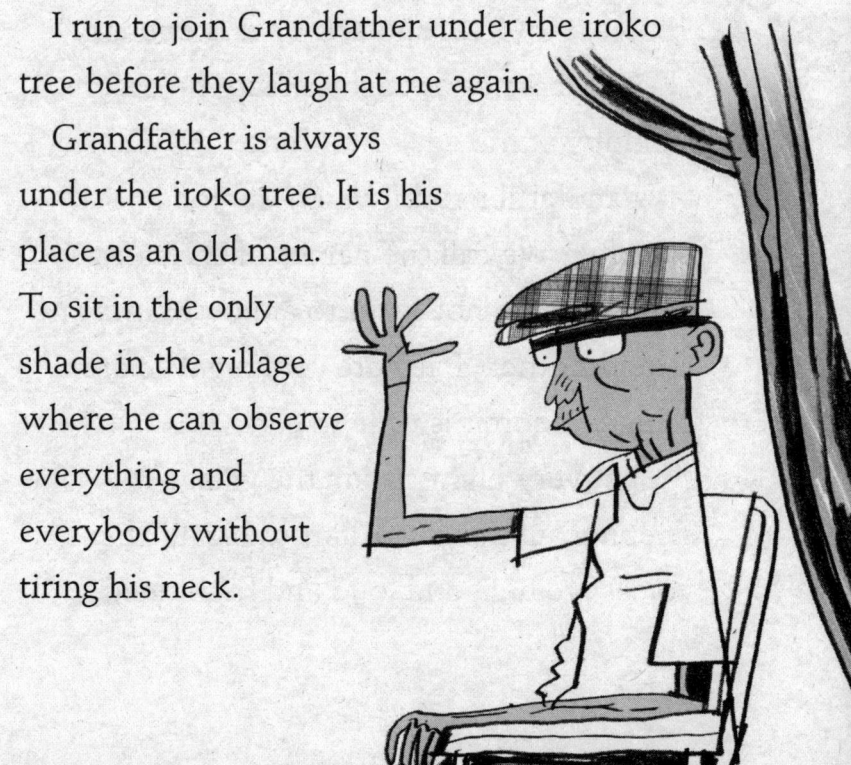

"You see that Firebird?" Grandfather asks me when I sit down. "A No. 1 car! And it is the only one in our country!"

I say nothing. Grandfather looks over at Sissy and the others. They are hitting a small rock with their catapults. That is not something I can do. Grandfather sighs.

"Nobody is good at everything, No. 1," he says. "You are the No. 1 car spotter. That is enough."

But it is not enough to stop the others laughing at me.

Grandfather and I watch the road together. We call the names of the cars softly. We do not want to annoy Mama and Grandmother. They are cooking. We are hungry. Soon it is time to eat.

That very night, when the village is sleeping, all the goats start to bleat. Their voices are high and loud and frightened.

Uncle Go-Easy's voice shouts out.
Then Mama Coca-Cola's. We jump up
from our mats. There is silence.
Slowly we lie back down.

In the morning we gather under
the iroko tree to hear
what has happened
in the night.

"A leopard! A great spotted leopard!" Uncle Go-Easy's voice shakes.

A leopard had visited his compound. It tried to take a goat but the speedy catapult of Tuesday deterred it. Then it went to Mama Coca-Cola's compound, where it succeeded. Now she has one less goat.

"This boy was sleeping." Mama Coca-Cola shakes Coca-Cola by his ear. "Where was his catapult?"

Our compound walls are not strong. They are made of brushwood, rotting planks and clay. Strong enough to pen goats in but not strong enough to keep leopards out.

Usually leopards like to keep as far from us as we do from them. It is a mutual understanding.

"This one must be old," says Grandfather.

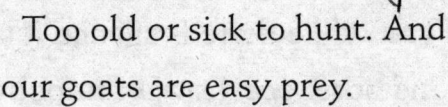

"Or sick," says Grandmother.

Too old or sick to hunt. And our goats are easy prey.

"The last time a leopard came we got rid of it," Mama says.

"But we had a whole village full of people then," Grandmother sighs.

"We lit torches and ran out of our houses, shouting and banging drums," Grandfather explains. "The leopard ran away."

"Now what will we do?" asks Aunty Fine-Fine. "Everybody is in the city and there are not enough of us left to frighten a leopard away."

"My goats will die-o! All of them!" wails Mama Coca-Cola. "Then I will be poor! Poor!"

"We have our catapults," says Tuesday.

"It is true!" agrees Uncle Go-Easy. "Tuesday succeeded in frightening off the leopard with his catapult last night!"

For a while there is silence. Then Grandfather speaks. "Let nobody go alone to the bush or the farm until this trouble is resolved," he says. "We will send word around to the other villages. They will come to help us chase the leopard away. Until then the children can fire their catapults, but only from the windows!"

Everybody nods in agreement.

I am glad Sissy is in my compound to fire catapult. If the leopard was as big as a hippopotamus, I would not be able to hit it.

"But what about me?" wails Mama B. "I have no child in the house that can fire catapult! The leopard will take all my goats."

It is true. Mama B's children are small.

"You can have Sissy," Mama says quickly.

I look at Mama wide-eyed but I say nothing. It is organized that every compound has a child old enough to shoot a catapult. Sissy goes to Mama B. And that leaves only me to protect our goats.

That night I wait by the window. I fire a stone from my catapult. It hits the wall. It does not even exit the window. Now it is Mama who looks at me wide-eyed.

Suddenly a leopard screams. Triumphant shouts come from Mama Coca-Cola's compound. Then our goats bleat loud and frightened. Grandmother wakes.

"Shoot, No. 1!" she shouts. "Shoot!"

A stone shoots from my catapult and exits the window. Hooray! But it is a goat that squeals and Mama snatches the catapult from me.

"Do you want to join the leopard in killing our goats!" Mama shouts.

Grandmother turns to Grandfather. He has his eyes tight shut.

"The leopard is stealing our goats and this boy can do nothing!" she wails.

"I am sleeping-o!" Grandfather mutters crossly. "Can an old man not sleep in his own house? The boy is old enough to look after things."

Mama turns away from the window. "The leopard has just taken one of our goats," she says.

Grandmother cries.

The following day Mama and Grandmother and I try to strengthen the compound walls. Sissy comes to help us. We bring more brushwood. That night the leopard comes again. This time my hands shake so badly I drop the stones. And the leopard carries off another goat.

The following night as we are eating, Grandmother wails.

"This boy is useless. Usless! We must ask Sissy to return."

We all look hopefully at Grandfather. He dips his cassava dough eba in some hot chilli pepper soup and lifts it to his mouth.

"And leave Mama B alone with three babies?" he asks. He shakes his head. Unthinkable.

We sell goats when we need money. But our goats will soon be gone. Our family will sink into poverty. And it will be all my fault.

I stretch out my hand to dip my eba into the stew. But I am thinking about our goats and I make a mistake. My hand copies Grandfather's and dips into the hot chilli pepper soup instead. Immediately I put the eba in my mouth, I am on fire.

"ARRRRRGGGHHH!!!!!!!!!!"

Grandmother and Grandfather are fond of the soup made of ground chilli peppers but children cannot eat it. One has to get used to it gradually, over years and years.

I run to the bucket and pour water into my mouth. Still my lips and tongue and throat are on fire.

Mama milks a goat. Grandfather pours milk into my mouth. Gradually the flames die down but the embers are still burning.

Grandmother sucks her teeth.

"Soon there will be no goats to save you from your own mistakes," she says. "Why do you not make the leopard run and scream instead of you!"

I look at Grandmother. Losing goats is making her mean. But her words have given me a No. 1 idea!

When everybody goes into the house to sleep I take one of Grandfather's old shirts that is outside drying. I fold the shirt and tie it tight around a goat. The goat bleats angrily.

"What is happening with that goat?" Mama's voice calls.

"I am collecting more milk for my throat," I answer hoarsely.

I take the soup pot. Quickly I smear the chilli pepper soup onto the shirt tied around the goat. The folded cloth prevents the paste from touching the goat's skin. But still

she bleats, annoyed. I tie her quickly to the fence. She bleats again.

"No. 1! Leave that goat and come inside!" Mama calls again.

I go inside and lie down on my mat. I close my eyes. No more waiting at the window with my catapult for me.

"Useless boy," Grandmother says.

In the middle of the night our goats begin to bleat. I recognize each one. Louder than all the others is the goat that is annoyed at wearing a shirt and being tied to the fence. I hear the creak of brushwood. The leopard is pushing its way into our compound!

I leap from my mat and press my face against the window. Let it choose the goat that is bleating so loud! Let it choose the one that cannot run!

I see the leopard spring. Then I hear it howl. It chose the right goat! Now it has tasted chilli pepper. My plan has succeeded!

Grandfather, Grandmother and Mama leap up and press their faces to the window. The leopard is rolling on the ground. I know that pain exactly. My own mouth is still hot.

"Sorry-o," I whisper.

"Sorry what!" shouts Grandmother. "What happen?"

"The leopard tasted pepper soup," I say.

Everybody looks at me.

"Pepper soup?" says Mama.

"I put a shirt onto a goat," I say. "And I put pepper soup on the shirt."

"You did what!" shouts Grandmother.

"The leopard tried to taste that goat but he tasted pepper soup first," I conclude.

Grandmother, Grandfather and Mama look back at the leopard. It is still rolling on the ground.

Suddenly the leopard leaps up. It crashes through the fence and races away into the night.

And our goat is running around the compound, still alive! And still wearing Grandfather's shirt!

Mama starts to laugh. She laughs so hard she cannot stop. Grandfather and Grandmother are laughing too.

"That leopard will not want to taste goat again," Mama says at last.

"And it will never enter a village again," chuckles Grandfather.

"I knew this boy was cleva!" Grandmother announces. "He is a cleva-cleva boy!"

"You said he was useless." Mama is still laughing.

"With the catapult that is true!" answers Grandmother.

"There is no need to be good with catapult," Grandfather says loudly, "when you have a No. 1 brain! Tomorrow we will tell your sister and those

other big hunters how you chased away
a leopard without using even a catapult."

That will stop them laughing at me,
I thought.

I smile my No. 1 smile. I am No. 0 at
catapult, but I am the No. 1 car spotter. And
I am No. 1 at chasing away leopards too!

No. 1 and the Flood

In my village Sissy is No. 1 at school, Coca-Cola is No. 1 at counting, Tuesday is No. 1 at catapult, Emergency is No. 1 at running, Nike is No. 1 at catching chickens, and I am the No. 1 car spotter.

Grandfather says there is no need to be No. 1 at more than one thing. That way we need one another. Call it co-operation. Call it friendship. If we were all No. 1 at everything we would no longer have any use for each other. And then what would be the point of being a human race?

All I wish is that the Firebird would cooperate with me. I am the No. 1 car spotter. And the Pontiac Firebird is the No. 1 car on our road. But I have never taken a good look at it. The professor who drives it has never stopped in our village.

Sissy thinks this does not matter. And Nike agrees. But they are girls. What do they know?

For Grandfather and Uncle Go Easy and the others, it is enough that such a No. 1 car passes by our village.

But I know that the day the Firebird stops here would be the No. 1 of all No. 1 days.

I am looking for dry firewood. In the rainy season it is hard to find. When it rains day and night everything is wet. But Grandmother has told me not to come back to the compound without dry wood. How else is she supposed to cook my food?

"No. 1! No. 1! No. 1!" Sissy is shouting.

She went this morning to the river to wash clothes. And when I look, I see Sissy and Nike are on the big rock. They like to wash clothes on this rock. It is on the edge of the water. Between the road and the river. You can climb the rock without getting your feet wet.

But now I see that the rock is surrounded by water on every side. All this rain has caused the river to swell. And here, where the road runs alongside the river, it is beginning to flood. I start to run.

"No. 1! Hurry up!" Nike shouts.

The river is not running fast. Sissy and Nike can both swim, but not with baskets full of wet clothes. And if we lose those clothes, we will have only the ones we are wearing. I prepare myself to swim to the rock and help Sissy and Nike.

But when I enter the water it does not even reach my knees. The girls jump off the rock and wade back to the road. I laugh at them.

"Did you call me because you were afraid to wet your feet?" I ask.

"We did not see the water rise," Sissy says.

"It could have been deep!" says Nike.

Of course they are right. And as we stand there the river swells more. Soon it has covered the whole road. The water is not moving fast. It looks like a small lake.

"Honda!" Coca-Cola shouts from the village.

The driver brakes when she comes around the corner and sees the flooded road. But when she notices that the water is only ankle deep, she drives through.

"Ford!" shouts Grandfather under the iroko tree.

"Peugeot!" shouts Emergency in the yam fields.

When the drivers see the flood, they too slow down and slowly-slowly pass. But the river continues to rise. Now it has reached my knees. It is as high as the foothold on the big rock.

"Limousine!" shouts Coca-Cola.

"BMW!" Emergency shouts.

The cars brake sharp on the edge of the flood. They look at the water swirling around our knees.

A big woman in an embroidered buba and wrappa gets out of the back of the limousine. A man in a sharp-sharp American suit gets out of the BMW. They greet each other loudly.

"Mammy-wagon!" calls Coca-Cola.

The mammy-wagon stops too. The bus driver climbs down. His passengers follow him, all looking agitated.

"O-ya! What now?" shouts a big man. "We are already late for our daughter's wedding because of your go-slow bus! Continue!"

"Oga-sir," begs the bus driver. "That water will quench my engine-o."

"You are making excuses!" shouts one of the women.

"We will miss the wedding. We will miss it-o!" the passengers wail.

"No. 1! No. 1!" Grandfather is shouting from the village. "What happen there?"

I turn and run back. As I run past Mama Coca-Cola's akara stall I shout: "The river done flood! The road is blocked! The cars cannot pass!"

Mama Coca-Cola's eyes shine. She puts four frying pans on the fire and calls to Mama B and Aunty Fine-Fine.

"Come and help me here! Come, my sisters-o! We will make money today!"

I run up to the iroko tree. I tell Grandfather about the flood.

"Let us go down!" says Grandfather.

Down at the flood all the people from the bus are crying and shouting into their mobile phones. I can see another bus on the other side of the water. It too has passengers who are waving their arms and shouting. The water is still no higher than the foothold on the rock, no deeper than my knee. But that is too deep for a car or bus to pass. These people are going nowhere.

Then I see something that makes me jump for joy. The Firebird. The fabulous Pontiac Firebird. It is approaching the flood. It will stop! At last it has to stop!

"Firebird!" I say to Grandfather.

He straightens his hat and straightens his back. I am dancing and jumping for joy.

The Firebird stops. There is only one person inside. It must be the professor. Grandfather has told me all about university professors. He has explained the whole thing to me.

"There are businessmen in this country and there are politicians. Most of them are corrupt. They are only interested in getting richer and richer!" he had said.

"Then there are those who help others. They have nothing dodgy going on. They put nothing into their pockets that belong to others. That is why we call them NGO, Nothing Going On. Like our own NGO, who gave us the wheelbarrows.

"The ones who teach the teachers and the doctors and the NGOs, those are the university professors! And the man who drives the Firebird?

He is one of those. A university professor."

I have never seen a university professor. Will he look like a politician in the embroidered robes of a chief or a businessman in a sharp-sharp American suit?

The door of the Firebird opens. A short man comes out and frowns at the flood.

He is not dressed like an American.

He is not dressed like a chief.

He is dressed like an ordinary man.

In traditional trousers and long matching shirt. Only the cloth that is new and fine shows he is not a poor man.

"Prof!" calls the chief from the limousine. "Don't tell me now that we politicians don't need our private planes!"

"Prof!" calls the businessman from the BMW. "How we can do business in this country when nobody repairs the roads?"

The people from the bus all turn to look at the people calling from their fine-fine cars.

"Can't you help us, madam chief?" One of the women begs the woman in the limousine.

Suddenly my mouth opens. Without consulting my brain.

"The water is not too deep," I say. "Why do you not walk to the other side?"

There is a short silence. The rich people laugh and the wedding people start to shout.

"You want us to spoil our clothes!"

"And arrive at the wedding looking like dogs!"

"Who asked you to talk to us? Were we talking to you?"

I look at the ground. My skin is crawling with shame.

"Whose foolish boy is this?" asks the lady chief.

A hand grips my arm.

"This is my boy, my No. 1 boy," says Grandfather. "Give him a problem and he will find a No. 1 solution."

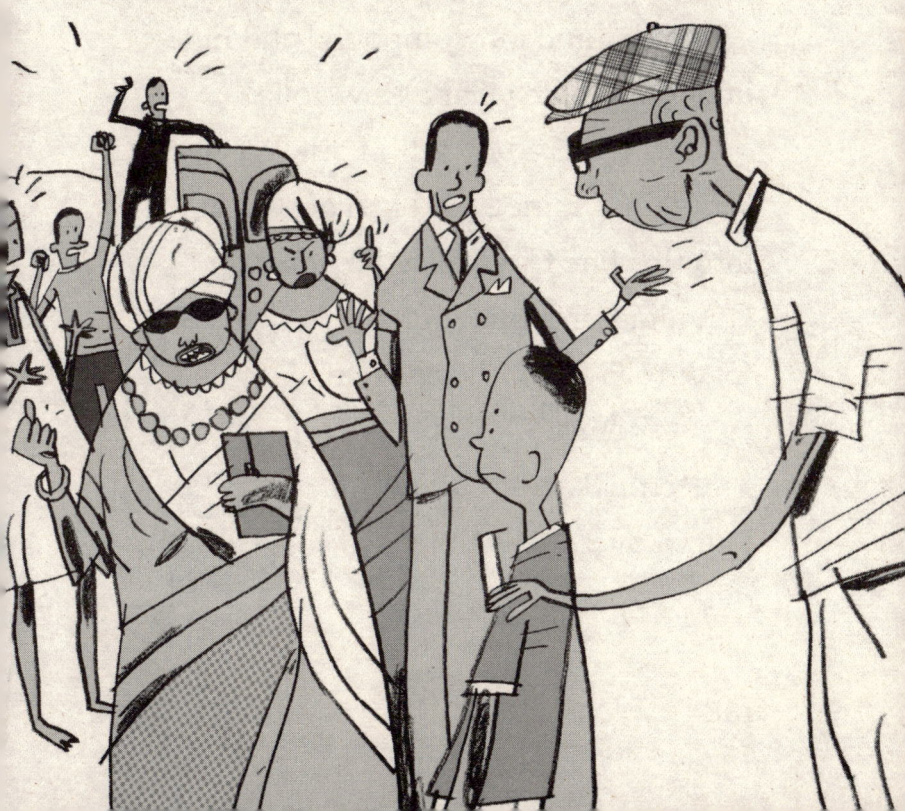

The professor raises his eyebrows. The rich businessman and the chief laugh. The people from the bus suck their teeth. What can a small boy like me do to solve a problem as big as this?

"These people cannot walk," Grandfather says to me. "You must use your No. 1 brain to find another solution."

But my brain is away from its desk. It has resigned. Everybody laughs as I run away.

I run behind our compound and hide underneath the village Cow-rolla.

Once I was a boy who achieved electricity for brain. I turned a broken down car into this fine Cow-rolla. I made Grandfather proud. But a Cow-rolla is not the answer to everything. Or is it?

Electric flash for brain! I jump over the wall into our compound.

"What are you doing?" shouts Grandmother. "Trying to give me a heart attack?"

I do not answer. I yoke the cows. I lead them from the compound.

"Where are you going with those cows? No. 1, answer me!" Grandmother is still shouting.

But the current is running and there is no off switch. Without answering I hitch the cows to the Cow-rolla and lead them away.

Grandmother is looking over the compound wall.

"Nobody will marry that boy. He is too much initiative-initiative," she grumbles.

"He will never listen to his wife."

I take the cows straight to the river. Now there are many cars and buses and people stopped on both sides of the flood. A little to one side is Grandfather.

As soon as he sees me, Grandfather smiles. Then he jumps up and shouts,

"Make way! Make way for the No. 1 river transport!"

Grandfather's hat falls into the water and the river carries it away but he does not notice. He is too busy shouting and waving his arms. Enjoying watching people's faces as they turn and see me arrive with the Cow-rolla.

"My No. 1 boy will take all of you to the other side of the water. The buses there can take you on your way." Grandfather shouts, "Show them, No. 1!"

I lead the Cow-rolla into the flood. The water only reaches the knees of the cows. There is no current. They are ready to cross.

Everybody is cheering and unloading their bags and baggages from the buses. The big people from the fine-fine cars push their way to the front.

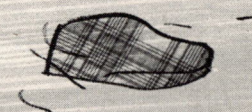

"What about us?" they ask. "How will we get our cars across?"

"Sorry," says Grandfather, "we only have public transport solutions here. People with private cars and private aeroplanes have to find their own way. Unless you want to take the bus?"

The rich go back to their cars. It is then that I see the Firebird is gone. The professor must have turned around to leave the way he came. He saw me run in shame. Did he see me return? I turn to Grandfather.

"One thousand naira per person," Grandfather is saying loudly to the people pushing to get onto the Cow-rolla. "Five hundred naira per bag."

People argue and complain but Grandfather refuses to move from the price.

"First you call my grandson foolish, you laugh at him and insult him. And now you want him to carry you back and forth, back and forth for nothing?"

Grandfather sucks his teeth. "No chance."

People dig into

their pockets. Those going to the wedding are the quickest to pay. I lead them across the flood on the back of the Cow-rolla. There they enter one of the buses waiting and go on their way. I come back carrying people who want to go this way. For many hours I lead the Cow-rolla through the water, back and forth. Sometimes my friend Coca-Cola walks with me. Sometimes my sister Sissy. They smile big smiles and wave to the people clicking us on mobile phone.

Grandfather collects handful after handful of notes. Grandmother cries with joy as she counts the notes at the end of the day.

"We will buy many-many more good fat strong goats with this money!" Grandmother says.

"To replace the ones the leopard took."

She is happy too that at last Grandfather has lost the disreputable hat his brother sent long ago from overseas.

The whole village comes to celebrate our wealth with us. Mama Coca-Cola too has made enough money to replace the goat the leopard took from her.

I hear many shouts of joy from my compound and from the whole village.

"Well done, No. 1! Well-done-o!"

That is what I hear.

It makes me happy. But what of the professor, what does he think of me?

Mama Coca-Cola's New House

I am the No. 1 and my best friend is Coca-Cola.

As you already know, Coca-Cola's mother, Mama Coca-Cola, runs the akara stall on the road. She cooks the best black-eyed bean akara fritters I have ever tasted. Buses, taxis, cars – many of them stop to buy Mama Coca-Cola's delicious akara. The stall is a good place to spot cars.

"Firebird!" Coca-Cola yells. He looks at me. "Come now. Shout!"

I say nothing. The Firebird passes, spraying water from the puddles on the road.

Mama Coca-Cola sucks her teeth.

"I will have to go and find plastic to cover this akara," she says. "When will this rainy season finish?"

I go to sit with Grandfather under the iroko tree. Together we watch the cars and buses drive past, spraying water everywhere. It is raining again.

Then Mama Coca-Cola's voice shouts from her house. "Bucket! Quick! Bring me bucket!"

I look at Grandfather.

"Go! Go!" he says.

I run to our compound and snatch Grandmother's buckets. I run to Coca-Cola's compound through the rain. Water is pouring through the roof of Mama Coca-Cola's house. And Mama Coca-Cola is rushing around trying to cover sacks of beans with small pieces of plastic.

"My beans!" she is shouting. "My beans will spoil!"

This is serious. How can Mama Coca-Cola cook akara without beans? And how will she feed her family if she does not sell akara?

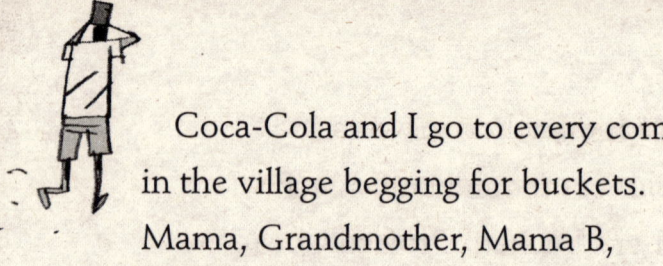

Coca-Cola and I go to every compound in the village begging for buckets. Mama, Grandmother, Mama B, Auntie Fine-Fine, Uncle Go-Easy and everybody comes to help. All that day we fight the rain. Moving buckets around the house, chasing the leaks that jump from one place to another. At last the rain stops. It is already night. Time to cook and sleep. Grandmother and Auntie Fine-Fine stretch and groan.

"Collect the buckets," Mama says to me.

"Let us go," says Mama B.

"Wait!" Mama Coca-Cola shouts. "Where are you going? I need those buckets! What will I do when the rain comes again?"

"You cannot expect our buckets to remain here throughout the rainy season!" Grandmother answers.

"My children are hungry and I need to cook," says Mama B. "I need to wash my vegetables, soak my beans and clean my yam. I need my buckets, sister."

Grandfather arrives at Mama Coca-Cola's compound.

He asks crossly, "Am I the only one in this village whose stomach knows it is time to chop?"

"She has our buckets!" Aunty Fine-Fine complains.

"They want my house to fall down and my beans to spoil!" Mama Coca-Cola shouts.

Grandfather sighs. He listens to everybody. Then he looks at Mama Coca-Cola's house.

It is a traditional house with palm leaf roof and round clay walls. But now it is old and cracked and leaky.

"The village must build Mama Coca-Cola a new house," Grandfather says at last.

It takes a whole village to build a house. It means women and girls digging and stamping and shaping mud into bricks for many long days. It means men and boys climbing and cutting and carrying and fixing sharp palm fronds for the roof. It means finding and stirring and mixing the exact traditional recipe for the plaster. It means everybody else cooking and cooking and cooking for those who are working so hard.

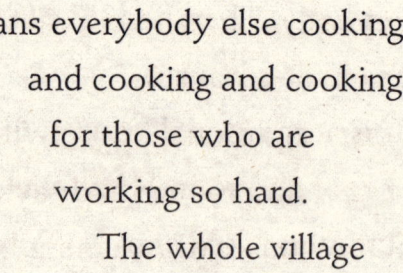

The whole village groans.

"There are not enough of us to build a house," Grandmother complains. "It takes a full village."

"Still, a house needs to be built," says Grandfather.

We all look at Mama Coca-Cola's house. Traditional houses cannot last, last, last. Not like the modern buildings I see in the town on market days. Nothing can wash away cement. Nothing can nibble away concrete. It does not crack. It is hard like iron.

"We cannot build now anyway," says Uncle Go-Easy. "If we build before the dry season comes, the rain will wash the clay bricks away."

"Then I must keep your buckets!" Mama Coca-Cola says crossly.

I clear my throat. Nobody looks at me. So I open my mouth and say, "If we build a modern house from cement blocks, then we can begin at once. And it will never leak."

"No. 1! Be quiet!" says Mama.

Children are not allowed to enter the conversations of their seniors. Especially not when serious matters are being discussed.

"Anyway, modern houses are expensive," says Grandmother.

"Too expensive for village people!" says Uncle Go-Easy.

Everybody nods. Then Grandfather says, "Mama Coca-Cola and her beans must stay with Mama B until the dry season. Then we can build her another house. Now, everybody, take your buckets and go and cook! I'm hungry!"

So Mama Coca-Cola moves her family and all her belongings, including her sacks of beans, to her sister, Mama B's, house. And we all return to our own compounds with our own buckets.

In the morning I can spot the road from where I am busy picking palm nuts high in the palm trees.

Mama Coca-Cola is busy at the akara stall. She is busy, not only frying akara, but also collecting money from every customer that owes her.

"Pay my money or else no more akara! No more!" I can hear her shout at every car, bus, lorry and taxi that stops.

Commuters, lorry drivers, taxi drivers, I see everybody pay. Once a person has tasted Mama Coca-Cola's akara, who can live without it?

When Mama Coca-Cola has finished collecting her money, she enters a taxi and sets off for the town. When she returns in the evening, Mama Coca-Cola is smiling wider than she has ever smiled before.

Now Mama Coca-Cola borrows mobile phone from everybody she knows who stops at the stall. She shouts loud and long into those phones. Until the day a big lorry arrives and parks behind the akara stall.

The lorry is full of men and a lot of building materials. There are sacks of cement and plaster and sand. There are

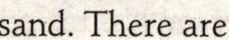

many-many concrete blocks. I quickly climb down from the palm tree, drop the nuts, and run to the road.

The whole village is gathered there staring at the modern expensive materials being unloaded right next to the akara stall. Mama Coca-Cola's smile is breaking her face.

"What is happening here?" Grandmother is puffing and panting.

"I am building a house," Mama Coca-Cola announces. "A fine *modern* house. Four concrete walls, four corners, iron roof, concrete floor. No more leaks. No more rain. Modern house, convenient life!"

Mama Coca-Cola looks at me.

"It is a No. 1 idea!" she says.

Grandmother sighs and shakes her head. She walks back to our compound.

"When you find a way for clothes to wash themselves, call me," she says over her shoulder. "Until then I am too busy for all this!"

I present myself to the builders. After all, this was my No. 1 idea and I am now ready to take part. But the builders laugh and shake their heads.

"This is not for small boys," they say. "Modern expertise is needed to build modern house."

The whole village laughs.

"No. 1!" Grandmother shouts from our compound. "I need firewood."

I pick up the sticks one by one as I watch those annoying ye-ye builders. They are clearing and digging the ground. What kind of modern expertise is that?

"No. 1!" shouts Grandmother. "Do you want to eat today or tomorrow?"

I return with the wood and stop under the iroko tree. Grandfather too is watching the builders. Now they are mixing powder from the sacks with water and sand to make a paste. I have helped to make a clay paste to build a traditional house.

"I can do that," I say to Grandfather.

"Concentrate on firewood," says Grandfather. "I want to eat today."

When I drop the firewood, Mama sends me to the river to water the cows. Uncle Go-Easy is there. Together we watch the house walls being built from big concrete blocks. The blocks are fixed together using the paste. We too use our clay paste to fix together small clay bricks.

"I can do that," I say.

"That is modern business," says Uncle Go-Easy. "Go easy, No. 1."

"And it is men's work," says Sissy, busy washing clothes. "Are you a man now?"

I narrow my eyes at Sissy but I say nothing more until later, when I am alone with Coca-Cola. It is siesta time. Everybody has returned to the compounds to eat and sleep. The builders are in Mama B's compound being fed by Mama Coca-Cola. Even Grandfather is absent from under the iroko tree.

"I can do everything those men are doing!" I say to Coca-Cola. "I can build your mother's house."

Coca-Cola looks at me with wide eyes. "You are truly the No. 1!" he says.

And Coca-Cola is truly my best friend.

"O-ya, come on!" I say.

Coca-Cola follows me down to the building site. There is a sack of white powder already open.

"Fetch water!" I say. "Pour!"

Coca-Cola tips a whole bucket of water onto the open sack. The powder flies up into the air and covers Coca-Cola and me from head to toe. All of a sudden we are white!

"Oyinbo!" I laugh at Coca-Cola. "White boy!"

Coca-Cola laughs too and pours more water onto the powder. The water sticks the powder to our feet. We begin to tread. This is the traditional way of forming a paste, mixing it with our feet. But there is too much water here. It runs along the ground, washing the powder away. I take another sack and empty it onto the mixture.

"We must work hard," I say to Coca-Cola, "and finish your mother's house before those lazy men wake up."

Coca-Cola and I work hard. But somehow the paste does not form well. And it is aggravating our feet. Burning them.

"Let us go to the river to wash," I groan. Coca-Cola agrees miserably.

But before we can go anywhere, my mother comes out of our compound. She takes one look at us and starts to scream. The whole village wakes up.

"No. 1! No. 1!" Mama wails. "Is that you?"

"It is him," says Sissy. "I recognize the shorts."

"Coca-Cola!" screams Mama Coca-Cola. "What has happened to my boy?"

Coca-Cola is crying, "My feet! My feet!"

I am crying too.

I cannot move ankle or toe.

Emergency runs to wake the sleeping builders.

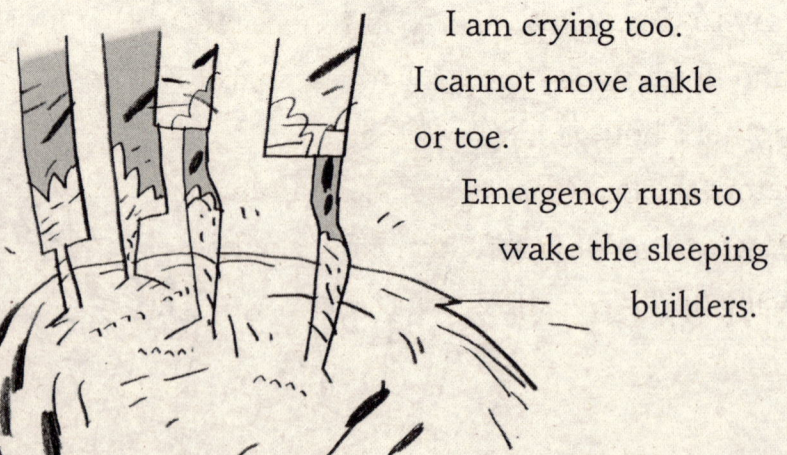

When they see Coca-Cola and me they laugh. They carry us down to the river.

The river washes the powdery cement easily off our bodies. But the cement that has hardened remains on our feet, burning our skin. The builders reassure us that eventually it will wear off. Our feet will only be white temporarily. But in the meantime our feet will pain us and Mama Coca-Cola will have to order some more materials to replace what we have wasted.

Mama Coca-Cola swings her handbag in the direction of Coca-Cola. Now she knows that he will live, she is angry.

"Now I will have to find more money!" she shouts. "Who told you to go and mix cement?"

"No. 1 did!" answers Coca-Cola sorrowfully.

"And if No. 1 told you to jump from a cliff, would you jump?" Mama Coca-Cola swings her bag at me.

"Just leave my boy alone!" shouts Mama.

Emergency carries me to sit under the iroko tree. Coca-Cola is brought there crying. Grandmother brings us ogi porridge and other sweet things to eat. She orders our mothers and all of the aunties not to ask me or Coca-Cola to do any work whatsoever. Because it might cause the cement to glue itself permanently to our feet.

"If those boys' feet are still white when they grow up NOBODY will marry them," Grandmother says.

I look at Coca-Cola. The pain in my feet is so bad, but if it means nobody will marry me, then I am happy. "Don't worry," I say to Coca-Cola. The food is good, the shade under the tree is pleasant, the company is superb, and there is an excellent view of the road… "Honda!" I shout happily.

Coca-Cola stops crying. He too looks at the road.

"Peugeot!" he shouts.

Sissy passes with a load of firewood on her head.

"Lazy boys!" she says.

I ignore her. After all I am the No. 1 car spotter. And right now I am busy. Busy doing what I do best!

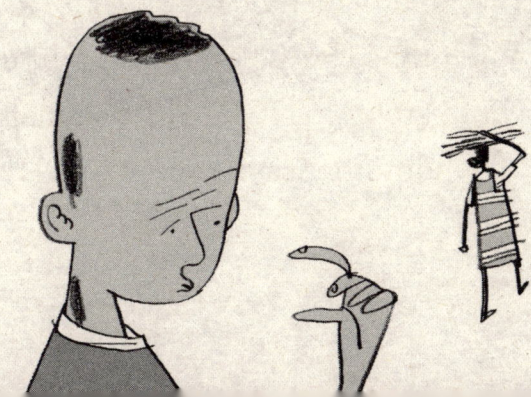

The No. 1 Chop-House

From where I sit under the iroko tree with Grandfather and Coca-Cola, I can keep my eye on everything. Coca-Cola and I still have cement on our feet, but not much. The burning has stopped. The pain has lessened. But we still cannot walk without help. We sit. We eat. We spot cars.

Down on the road Mama Coca-Cola's new house meets in four corners, just as Mama Coca-Cola has requested.

Grandmother sucks her teeth.

"Does Mama Coca-Cola not know that dust likes to hide in corner-corner?"

But it is too late for discussion. The builders are already attaching the strong sheets of corrugated iron roof.

"No more leaking! You see that iron? That is solid iron between me and the rain!" Mama Coca-Cola is so happy.

But Grandfather shakes his head. "I have seen many-many iron roofs with rust hole like colander admitting the rain. It is only a matter of time!"

But Mama Coca-Cola dances when her roof is completed. And claps as the builders plaster the walls inside and out.

"Why that white nonsense?" Grandfather asks. "Is our traditional plaster not good enough?"

But it is too late to argue. Mama Coca-Cola's house is finished! She is calling friends and family from all over the area to celebrate. And it is up to the village to provide a good feast.

From under the iroko tree we see Sissy pushing wheelbarrows of soft drinks and carrying sacks of beans ready for the party.

"Lazy-lazy boys," she hisses at us.

When I am alone I find that I can wiggle my toes. And Coca-Cola and I even enjoyed a game of football when everybody was away at market. Just for rehabilitation. But right now I am too busy spotting the cars of all Mama Coca-Cola's relatives and friends to answer Sissy.

At the party Coca-Cola and I are given good seats next to Grandfather. We are served good food. Amala and ewedu, Grandfather's favourite. Pounded yam and goat stew, Coca-Cola's favourite. Jollof rice and fried chicken, my favourite. I eat them all!

"Not too lazy to eat," Sissy hisses.

When the drums start, people begin to dance. I look down and suddenly I see my feet begin to move. I try to hide them under Grandfather's stool. But the drums continue, getting louder.

Before I know what I am doing, my feet enter the dance floor. Up and down and around they dance. Jumping and stamping, crouching and leaping high! Celebrating Mama Coca-Cola's new house.

"No. 1! No. 1!" Mama and Grandmother are cheering. "Our boy is cured!"

"Coca-Cola!" Mama Coca-Cola shouts happily. "Coca-Cola!"

Coca-Cola is there, dancing beside me. We dance so well that the drummers drum louder and faster for us.

I see Sissy narrow her eyes and when I leap into the air she shouts, "No. 1, your bom-bom is still white!"

I twist in the air to take a look at my bottom and everybody laughs! Quickly I sit down. Sissy smirks.

Now Mama Coca-Cola's new house is finished, the party is over, and life is as before. Coca-Cola and I are busy all day fetching and carrying, herding the goats, watering the cows, hoeing the fields, gathering palm nuts and carrying firewood. Mama, Grandmother and the aunties smile to see us work so hard. They say they are giving us all these jobs to help us rebuild our muscles after all that sitting down.

But there is one thing that is not as before. When I look towards the iroko tree, there is somebody sitting in my place next to Grandfather. It is Mama Coca-Cola. Ever since she moved to her new house, she has stopped frying akara and started sitting under the iroko tree.

"Your mother is under the iroko tree," I say to Coca-Cola one day when we are in the bush.

He shrugs.

"Does she not have akara to fry?" I ask.

"She has headache," Coca-Cola says.

I frown at Coca-Cola. Mama Coca-Cola never has a headache.

When we return to the village, I allow my legs to wander close to the iroko tree. I can hear Mama Coca-Cola's voice. "That iron roof like oven. OVEN! I tell you. All night I am sweating! Sweating! And come morning I have headache. BIG headache."

Grandfather shakes his head sorrowfully and waves his fly whisk.

"I cannot fry akara. My headache is too big," continues Mama Coca-Cola. "And I cannot even lie in my own house because it is hot-hot-hot. I have to sit here in the shade and watch my business die!"

Mama Coca-Cola starts to cry. Then Coca-Cola starts to cry. Sunshine and Smile, sitting at their mother's feet, start to cry. The women come out of their compounds and gather around Mama Coca-Cola.

"That house is dirty! Dirty! No matter how many times I sweep, every time I look in corner I find dust! And Coca-Cola is coughing-coughing all night."

I look at Coca-Cola. "Why did you not tell me?" I ask.

Coca-Cola shrugs.

He does not meet my eye. And I know why. This house was my idea.

"This is very bad," says Grandmother.

"But it is worse. Look at my babies!" Mama Coca-Cola cries.

Mama Coca-Cola holds up Sunshine and Smile. They are covered in angry red bites.

"Mosquitoes love my house!" Mama Coca-Cola wails. "They love it too much!"

"This is not good!" cries Grandmother. "Your babies will become sick!"

"It is very bad." Mama Coca-Cola weeps.

Nobody knows what to say. This is terrible. And it is all my fault. The fault of my bad idea, that now my tight friend and his family are suffering.

A BMW races past the abandoned akara stall, splashing it with water from the road. One of the crates falls over into the mud.

Mama Coca-Cola weeps louder when she sees this. Mama tries to comfort her.

"When you are back in business, everybody will stop and buy," she says.

"Nobody with money ever stopped to buy from me," Mama Coca-Cola cries. "Rich people, they all want chop-house restaurant. They like to sit on chair, to enjoy four walls and a roof."

I look down at the akara stall. It is three upturned crates normally piled high with plates of akara. In the rainy season Mama Coca-Cola covers the plates with plastic to protect them from the rain. In the dry season she uses a small leafy branch to wave flies from the plates. Nobody ever stops there who is not happy to squat on the ground while they eat.

"It was not a good business anyway," Mama Coca-Cola sobs.

Everybody looks worried. Will Mama Coca-Cola abandon her business for ever?

Another car races along the road. It is the Firebird. I am too sad for Mama Coca-Cola to shout out. The Firebird slows down by Mama Coca-Cola's new house and then speeds up again. The professor probably mistook the new house for one of those fancy chop-house restaurants that rich people love so much.

This triggers electricity for brain! I am on my feet. "Chop-house! Chop-house!" I shout.

Everybody looks at me as if I have gone crazy. Uncle Go-Easy, who was squatting, falls over in the dust. Mama tries to shush me. "We do not need another of your ideas," she says.

I run down to the road. I take a big stick and point to the walls of Mama Coca-Cola's house. I shout loud so that everybody under the iroko tree can hear me.

"Four walls!" I say. "Like chop-house."

Grandfather stands up. He shades his eyes and looks towards the house.

I point to the roof.

"Roof!" I shout. "To protect customers from sun and rain."

Mama Coca-Cola is now standing too. And so are Mama and the aunties and even Uncle Go-Easy. They are all staring at the house.

I point to the concrete floor through the open door.

"Concrete floor!" I shout. "To support tables and chairs for those who do not like to squat on the ground."

Suddenly Mama Coca-Cola is running towards the house. The whole village is following her. When she reaches the house her eyes are wide. I point to the ground where I am standing, next to the house.

"Shade," I say quietly, "for somebody to fry akara out of the hot-hot sun."

Mama Coca-Cola closes her eyes. "But if this is a chop-house, where will I and my children sleep?"

"In my house," says Mama B quickly. "You must return to my house."

"And when the rainy season is over, we will build you a new house," says Grandfather.

"A traditional house," says Grandmother loudly, "with no corner for the dirt to gather. Palm frond roof and thick clay wall to keep the house cool and quiet."

"And traditional plaster that soothes the eyes and repels the mosquitos," says Uncle Go-Easy.

Mama Coca-Cola smiles and then laughs. Then she shouts, "Coca-Cola! Run for town! Tell the sign painter to come here. Tell him I want red, yellow, green and plenty-plenty words."

Mama Coca-Cola looks at us. "I need tables. I need chairs. You must lend me yours. I will return them when I have money to buy my own," she says.

The aunties groan.

"And when I return them, I will buy everybody one new chair," Mama Coco-Cola continues.

"First our buckets, now our tables and chairs," Grandmother says crossly.

But everybody goes to their houses and carries any tables or chairs they own down to the new chop-house. We all want to help Mama Coco-Cola. Who does not want a rich chief to sit on their chair and eat at their table?

Now only three days later we have a brand new modern chop-house on the road outside our village. For those who can read, the sign says:

The smell of frying akara speaks to those who can't read.

In the shade near the door, Mama Coca-Cola is frying akara and chatting to those customers who prefer to squat outside in the traditional way.

Next to them are parked BMWs and Mercedes Benz. The owners are enjoying akara inside. Sitting on chairs and eating at tables which were in our own houses not so long ago.

"Firebird!" shouts Coca-Cola.

The Firebird stops right outside the chop-house. The professor climbs out. He is holding a newspaper. He enters the chop-house. Coca-Cola comes running up to the iroko tree.

"The prof!" he shouts. "The prof is looking for you!"

I look at Grandfather. He looks at me. Then Grandfather stands up under the iroko tree and brushes the dirt from his clothes. He walks stiffly down to the road. Grandfather enters the chop-house. Coca-Cola and I follow him and look through the window. The professor greets Grandfather. They look at the paper the professor is holding. Grandfather smiles.

"No. 1!" he shouts.

I enter the chop-house. On the front of the newspaper is a photograph of me leading the Cow-rolla loaded with passengers through the flood!

"It seems I left too early and missed the fun." The professor smiles at me.

I smile back my biggest smile. Then I look out of the window at the Firebird. It is so close! The professor puts the paper down.

He laughs. "You are more interested in my car than your own celebrity photograph!"

I nod my head. The professor laughs again.

"Let us eat some of this famous akara!" he says. "I want to hear more about your ideas. Then I will take you for a ride in my car."

I smile a big-big smile. Some of my ideas are No. 1. And some are not. But no matter – I am the No. 1. The No. 1 car spotter in the world. I can eat akara with a university professor, no problem!

Then I am going to jump into the fabulous Pontiac Firebird! I am the No. 1 car spotter – now watch me cruise in the No. 1 car!

THE N°1 CAR SPOTTER
and the Car Thieves

by Atinuke

illustrated by Warwick Johnson Cadwell

Walker Books

For Mama Akara —
and all of the ancestors
who live on in me and my boys
A.

To my gang as ever,
D, S, H and W
W.JC.

The No. 1 Car Spotter in the Palm Tree

Heh – look up in the palm tree!

Is me! Oluwalase Babatunde Benson, otherwise known as No. 1, *the* No. 1!

You remember this bush village where I live? You remember my friends Coca-Cola and Emergency and Tuesday? You remember Grandmother and Grandfather? And Mama? And my sister Sissy? I can point them all out to you from up here in the tree. Look!

See Coca-Cola, pushing his wheelbarrow of soft drinks up from the river to his mother, Mama Coca-Cola. She is busy frying akara at her No. 1 chop-house road-side restaurant.

Emergency and Tuesday are throwing nets into the river with their father, Uncle Go-Easy! Their sister, Nike, and my sister, Sissy, are carrying firewood back to our cooking fires!

Grandfather is observing everybody and everything from the shade of the iroko tree. And Grandmother, Mama and the aunties are busy with the new palm oil press!

From high up in this palm nut tree I can see the village, I can see the river, I can see the bush. And most important of all, I can see the road! And all the fine-fine cars that pass.

"Mercedes-Benz ML 320! Peugeot 505! VW Jetta!"

I know them by their engines before I even see them. That is why I am called No. 1. I am the No. 1 car spotter in my village. I spot all cars. I shout their names. And when Mama Coca-Cola hears me shout, she turns up the cooking fires.

By the time the vehicles near the chop-house, the smell of frying chicken and akara and goat meat has fully penetrated the air conditioning systems of the vehicles.

The cars brake. They stop right outside the No. 1 chop-house. The drivers cannot help themselves. Their stomachs are now ruling the brake pedal. The people in the Mercedes and the Jetta jump out and go into the chop-house.

It is thanks to me that Mama Coca-Cola has a chop-house. Thanks to me Mama Coca-Cola now has customers who drive Mercedes-Benz. This means she can charge more than ten times the amount for her

akara than she could before, when her customers had to squat by the side of the road. And now that Mama Coca-Cola is making good money, come January, my tight friend Coca-Cola will be able to go to school! He will learn ABC. He will learn 1-2-3 – just like you – and when he grows up he will be a big man!

I am so happy for my best friend Coca-Cola. I am so proud of him. When he is a big man, we will live together in the city in his fine house and we will continue our car spotting. But instead of spotting cars on the road, we will be spotting cars parked in his own garage! BMW! Land Cruiser! Porsche!

"No. 1!" Grandmother shouts. "Are you picking palm nuts or are you catching flies?"

"He is spotting cars!" Sissy shouts back angrily under her load of firewood.

My sister Sissy thinks car spotting should be banned by the government.

She is angry that I am up in the cool breeze while she is sweating on the hot ground doing all the jobs that we normally share. Collecting firewood and water, grazing the goats in the bush, watering the cows at the river, sweeping the compound.

Sissy would rather be high in the cool trees picking palm nuts than down on the hot ground carrying heavy loads. But Grandmother says Sissy is a big girl now, too big to climb trees.

"No. 1!" Grandmother shouts again. "If you do not start picking palm nuts, you will be sleeping in that tree tonight. Because none of us are moving from here until my palm oil jars are full!"

I start to pick nuts quick-quick.

"Lamborghini DIABOLO!" I hear Coca-Cola screech.

My eyes turn immediately to the road. A bright red Lamborghini is flying towards the village!

Mama Coca-Cola turns up the fire and the speed machine slows. It parks in front of the chop-house. A woman in a white dress emerges.

With customers like this, Mama Coca-Cola will be able to charge twenty times the amount for her akara. She will be able to send Coca-Cola to school in the US of A!

Two men in blue suits leave the chop-house. I saw them when they jumped out of their Jetta. Now one jumps into the Jetta and the other jumps into the Lamborghini. They both drive off.

My mouth falls open.

"No. 1!" Grandmother shouts once more. "What is wrong with you?"

My lips move but no sound comes out.

The woman in white comes out of the chop-house. She looks at the place where she had parked her Lamborghini. She looks around. She starts to scream.

Emergency and Tuesday and Uncle Go-Easy have dropped their fishing nets. Grandfather is struggling to his feet. I slide down from the palm tree.

"No. 1!" Grandmother is still shouting. "I am warning you!"

"Quiet," says Grandfather as he hobbles over. "Something has happened here, something more important than palm oil."

Grandmother is speechless.

The police arrive. They question me. They question all of us. We all saw it happen. But we cannot help the police. None of us has ever seen the men in blue suits or the Jetta before.

Eventually the Lamborghini woman departs in a battered yellow taxi with its doors held on by rope.

"I will never eat here again! Never!" she shouts at Mama Coca-Cola.

The next morning, before the sun has even passed the horizon, I am back in the palm tree.

"Today I want to see palm nuts," Grandmother orders. "No matter if cars are stolen left, right and centre!"

Uncle Go-Easy, Emergency and Tuesday are picking palm nuts today too. Fish needs palm oil to fry. Coca-Cola is in the trees as well. Akara needs palm oil too.

Only Sissy and Nike are sweating on the hot ground. Sissy narrows her eyes and sucks her teeth.

It is so early in the morning even the road is slow. Only mammy-wagons rumble up and down. The one they call *Always Willing* stops first. Its passengers climb down to eat akara, squatting by the roadside.

Then cars start to pass.

"Peugeot 504," I whisper so Grandmother does not hear me. "Santana."

The cars park in front of the chop-house. People get out to buy akara. The men from the Peugeot eat in their car. I can see them busy on one tiny-tiny laptop.

"Honda Accord. Golf. Daewoo."

"*Rolls-Royce Phantom!*"

Our mouths are open, our hands are frozen.

A uniformed driver gets out and opens the back door of the Rolls. A big man in a chief's agbada robes enters the chop-house to sit on a chair and buy his akara at prices as inflated as his agbada. His driver goes around the back to buy his own akara at a more affordable price.

"Dat car shine pass Saturday night shoes!" Tuesday whispers. Grandmother looks up. We start to pick nuts again quick-quick. But I keep one eye on the chop-house. I have seen that chief before. In the newspaper!

In the Peugeot the two men are still busy on their laptop. Then one of them jumps out. He jumps into the Rolls. The Peugeot and the Rolls Royce drive off at top speed.

The akara falls out of the chief's driver's mouth.

"TIEF!" I shout. "TIEF! TIEF!"
People pour out of the chop-house. But by the time the chief emerges, his Rolls Royce is gone. There is only his driver running up the empty road with his mouth still open, trying to chase the cars.

I slide down the palm tree and jump to the ground. Coca-Cola, Emergency, Tuesday and Uncle Go-Easy all follow me. *Thump! Thump! Thump! Thump!* Like ripe fruits falling to the ground.

"Not again!" wails Grandmother.

When I tell the police what I saw, the chief shakes his fist at me. "Useless boy!" he shouts. "Why did you not stop them? Why did you not shout quicker?"

* * *

That night my brain is alive with electricity.
I whisper to Sissy. She shakes her head.

"You must be crazy," she whispers back.

But the current is flowing, and I have
no OFF switch. I keep whispering and
whispering until Sissy agrees.

The next day I am in the palm
nut tree before cock-crow.

Sissy is wandering along the
side of the road with the hungry
goats. If Grandmother sees her she
will send her into the bush, where
the sweetest grasses grow.

But Grandmother is fighting with the
palm oil press. It is refusing to work.

"Foolish machine!" Grandmother growls.

"What will we do?" cries Auntie Fine-Fine.

"We have not even finished paying for it!"
My mother has her head in her hands.

Then I see something.

"Firebird!" I shout.

"Firebird! Firebird!"

There is only one Pontiac Firebird in this our country. It is owned by a university professor. A man who stops in our village to eat akara and show us the newspapers. Once he even gave me a ride in his car!

"Firebird!" I shout again, ignoring Grandmother's narrowed eyes.

Following the Firebird is a Volkswagen Golf. Soon a Mercedes V-Boot and a Hummer HT3 join them in front of the chop-house.

Almost everybody gets out of their cars. Prof waves to me and I wave back. The men in the V-Boot are still in their car. They open a laptop.

Grandmother, Mama and the aunties are silent. They are looking at the broken palm oil press. The money we have spent on it is wasted and we haven't finished paying yet!

Suddenly I hear the Hummer's doors opening. A man jumps out of the V-Boot and into the Hummer.

The thieves gun their engines and speed away!

"TIEF! TIEF! TIEF!"

I shout as loud as I can.
Sissy hears me!

She drives the goats into the road right in front of the speeding cars. Grandmother screams.

"Don't worry!" I shout. "Sissy knows what she is doing!"

But the speeding cars do not slow down.

They drive straight into the goats.

Dust flies up everywhere.

I jump straight down from the tree SMACK! onto the hard ground. For one second I cannot breathe. Then I look up and see Sissy. She is lying by the side of the road. Grandmother and Mama are screaming.

"Sissy! Sissy! SISSY!"

I reach her first. I wrap my arms around my sister.

"Did we catch'am?" she whispers.

Grandmother and Mama are leaning over us.

"Who told you!" Grandmother screams at Sissy. "Who told you to do such a stupid thing?"

I hide behind Mama. Everybody has come running from the village to see if Sissy is OK.

"This boy!"

Grandmother is shouting for everybody to hear. She looks angrier than I have ever seen in my life.

"This boy asked my granddaughter to go and kill herself. For what? For a car! A *car*!"

"*Na-wa-oh*, mama!" says a bus driver.

Everybody looks at me. I hang my head and start to cry.

"We thought the thieves would stop if the goats blocked the road." Sissy is crying too.

"Unbelievable." The Hummer driver shakes his head. "These children are very brave."

"They just do not understand how bad people can be," says the professor sadly.

Suddenly Grandmother starts to cry as well!

The Hummer driver takes his wallet out of his pocket.

"Your grandchildren tried to save my car," he says to Grandmother. "Let me reward them."

Grandmother opens her mouth to refuse. But Mama points to the broken palm oil press. So Grandmother takes the money and puts it in her blouse for safe-keeping.

"God will bless you," she says to the driver.

He has lost his car and still he rewarded us.

Then Grandmother grabs my ear and leads me back to our compound.

Mama rubs Sissy with medicinal oil. Sissy was not hit by the cars. She was knocked over by the goats as they ran. One goat was killed.

"From now on," Mama says to Sissy, "you are back up in palm trees where I can keep my eye on you."

That night everybody eats goat meat apart from me. I am in the house alone, sitting on my mat.

Maybe that chief was right.

Maybe I am just
a useless boy.
A useless
village boy.

Then Sissy comes in with a bowl of food. "No. 1," she whispers. "Tomorrow Grandmother will remember that it was you who got the money to fix the palm oil press. You are truly the No. 1!"

"And tomorrow," Sissy continues "I will be the one in the cool trees and you will be the one collecting firewood."

Sissy smiles a big smile. It's so good to see my sister alive and smiling, I can't help it, I smile too. I smile my No. 1 smile!

No. 1 Opens His Big Mouth

I am No. 1 at spotting cars. Almost every day I spot another one stolen.
First I spot the thieves busy on their laptops. Then I spot them steal a car. How are they overriding the cars' security systems?

"A-beg, use that No. 1 brain," says Coca-Cola.

"Make we catch dese thieves!" says Tuesday.

"With one No. 1 plan!" says Emergency.

But the thought of Sissy lying in the dust has jammed my brain's operating system.

Anyway, what can a boy in a palm tree do against a man with a laptop?

Prof reads to us from the newspapers. It is not just here where cars are being stolen. "Cars are being stolen from all over the country," Prof says. "Cities and towns and villages, the same. It is a national problem. The chief of police himself is on the case."

Prof looks at me. "Don't let your friends vex you, No. 1. This is a rich man's problem. Do you people even have a car for thieves to steal?"

All of us laugh. The only car in our village broke down here and the owner never came to take it away. Thanks to one of my No. 1 ideas it is now the village cart.

But when Prof is gone the other boys keep on vexing me. Even Uncle Go-Easy, even Grandfather wants me to tackle those thieves.

"I don't know where you are hiding that No. 1 brain of yours!" says Uncle Go-Easy.

"You have more brains than all those thieves put together!" says Grandfather.

"O-ya," says Mama Coca-Cola. "You don't have to solve the whole national whatever, just stop the thieves from operating here."

"It is not my problem," I say.

Grandfather raises his eyebrows.

"It is a rich man's problem," I say.

"You think a problem can be one person's alone?" Grandfather asks me.

He shakes his head.

"What affects one of us affects us all. We are one human race!"

"I am only saying what Prof says," I say.

But maybe Grandfather is right. Every time a fine-fine car is stolen from outside the chop-house and the owner is forced to leave in a battered old taxi, it is Mama Coca-Cola that they blame.

"I will not eat here again!" they shout. "Useless ye-ye woman! Don't you know about security? Don't you have surveillance camera?"

Us, who do not even have electricity! It pains Mama Coca-Cola. It pains all of us.

Prof reassures her. "Cars are being stolen from outside all restaurants and schools, even hospitals!"

"So why do they blame me!" Mama Coca-

Cola wails.

"It will soon stop, it will soon stop," Prof says calmly. "The chief of police himself is on the case."

Mama Coca-Cola sucks her teeth. "I do not see the chief of police here."

"But he is widening the net, he is widening the net." Prof is reading from the newspaper.

"Is the chief of police a fisherman?" I joke. "If so, I hope he knows how to throw his net well-well. A speeding Mercedes is hard to catch."

Everybody laughs loud. Uncle Go-Easy stands up and pretends to throw an imaginary net.

"I go catch one million dollar fish!" he shouts.

Even Prof is laughing.

* * *

The next day I am down at the river, watering the cows. Uncle Go-Easy is catching fish with Emergency and Tuesday.

"TIEF! TIEF!" I hear Coca-Cola shout.

I turn towards the chop-house. A Range Rover Overfinch is speeding away. A fat man in a fine agbada is trying to run up the road.

The Range Rover is almost level with me now. I can see a man hunched over the wheel.

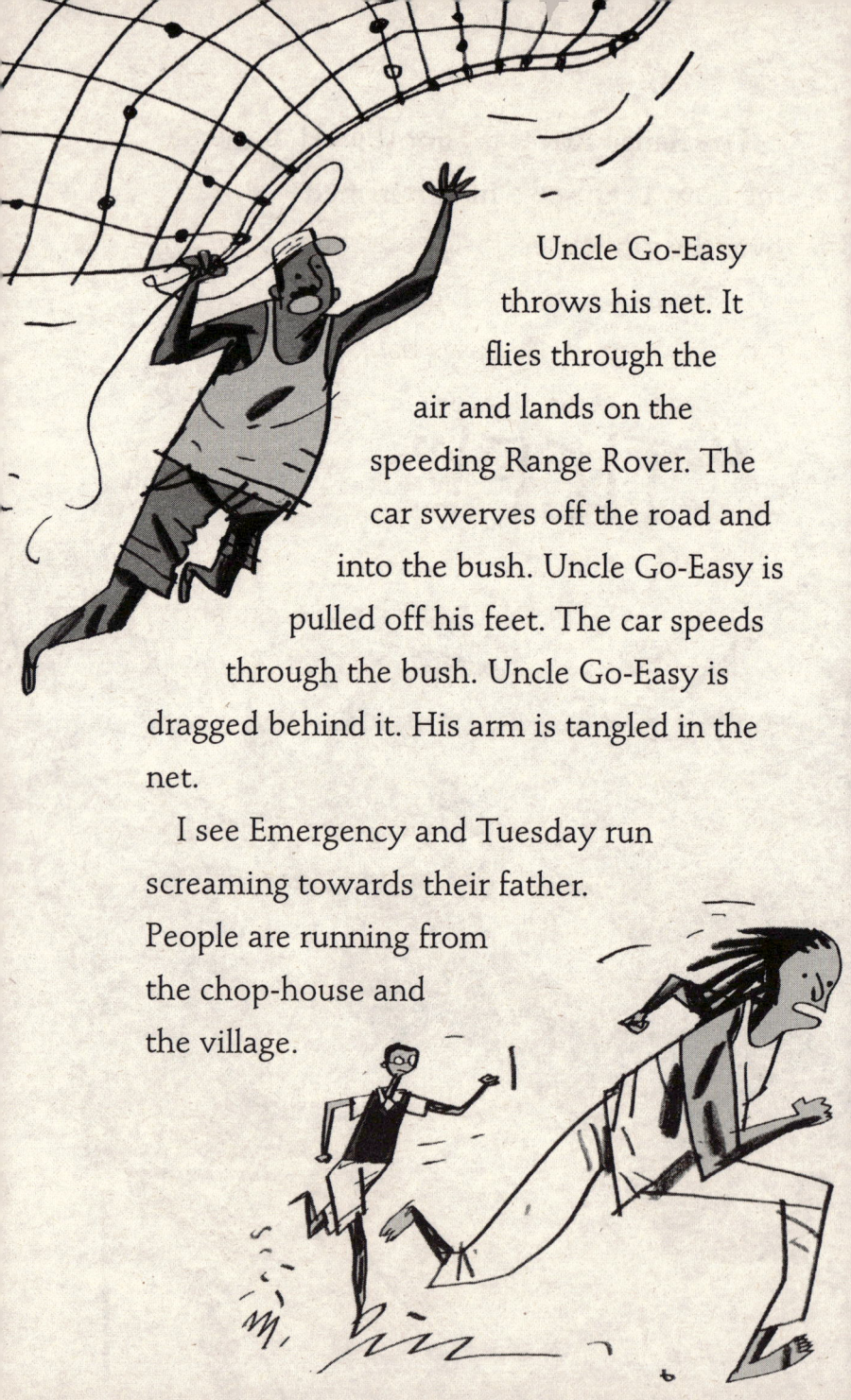

Uncle Go-Easy throws his net. It flies through the air and lands on the speeding Range Rover. The car swerves off the road and into the bush. Uncle Go-Easy is pulled off his feet. The car speeds through the bush. Uncle Go-Easy is dragged behind it. His arm is tangled in the net.

I see Emergency and Tuesday run screaming towards their father. People are running from the chop-house and the village.

I stand where I am. I see the net tear on a tree. I see the Range Rover drive back onto the road and away, fast. I see them carry Uncle Go-Easy to the village. I see blood.

Slowly I take the cows back to the compound. Grandfather is there.

"It is not your fault, No. 1!" he says.

I say nothing. I go into the dark house. I sit on my mat.

After a while I hear Mama and Sissy and Grandmother come in crying.

"They have taken him to the hospital," Mama says.

Then I hear Grandmother say, "Why does that boy have to put his stupid ideas into everybody's heads!"

I lie down on my mat. When my mother comes to call me for food, I do not answer her.

From now on I sit under the iroko tree with Grandfather. I do not talk. I do not laugh. I do not spot cars.

There are no good cars to spot anyway. The rich people have decided to stay at home. Whenever they go out, people steal their cars.

Mama Coca-Cola's chop-house is quiet now. She has plenty-plenty customers still. But only the ones who prefer to squat outside in the shade. Only the ones who can pay small-small for their food. The ten-times, twenty-times customers are at home, eating their own akara.

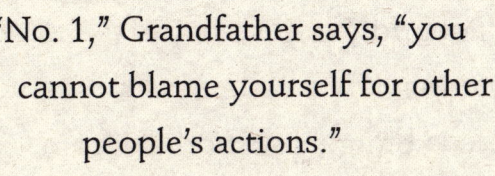

"No. 1," Grandfather says, "you cannot blame yourself for other people's actions."

But if I had not opened my mouth, Uncle Go-Easy would never have tried to catch a speeding car with his fishing net.

And he would not be in hospital now. And his daughter Nike would not be there looking after him.

And his sons Emergency and Tuesday would not be catching fish day and night to pay for medicine.

And Mama and Sissy would not be herding their goats and cows. Soon those goats and cows will have to be sold to pay for hospital bills. When Uncle Go-Easy comes out he will have nothing. And no matter what Grandfather says, I know it is the fault of my big mouth.

"Firebird!" It is Coca-Cola shouting.

He is bringing soft drinks from the river in his wheelbarrow for Mama Coca-Cola's customers. I know, and he knows, and Mama Coca-Cola knows, that unless the rich customers return, Coca-Cola will never go to school. He will not become a rich man and live in a fine house and drive his own car. He will push a wheelbarrow of soft drinks for the rest of his life.

Prof parks his car. He looks at the empty chop-house. He turns to where I am sitting with Grandfather under the iroko tree.

"I had thought this was only a rich man's problem," says Prof, "but I can see I was wrong."

Grandfather nods his head.

"One person's problem is always everybody's problem," he says.

"But what about the poor?" Prof asks. "When the poor suffer, they suffer alone."

Grandfather looks at Prof.

"You are an educated man," he says. "Your parents had the money to send you to school. And now you are in a position to help our whole country. But what if your parents had been poor. Would you even be able to help yourself?"

"But if I had been poor, who would have suffered apart from me?" Prof says.

"The whole country would have suffered!" Grandfather says loudly. "From the loss of a great teacher. Everybody you have ever taught would have lost.

"Everybody suffers from poverty. From the loss of teachers and doctors who could have saved lives, leaders and inventors who could have made lives better. Instead, those clever ones are struggling in poverty just to feed themselves. Maybe they have even become armed robbers and thieves!

"Believe me," says Grandfather. "The whole world suffers from poverty."

Prof is silent for a long time. He looks at the sky and the one cloud that is slowly passing and the goats that are chewing.

At last he says, "Baba, you are right. Why did my universities not teach me this? I have been to Harvard, to Oxford, to UniLag. Nobody spoke of this."

Grandfather laughs. "There is a difference between what is taught in the university and what an old man knows. One is education, the other is wisdom."

Grandfather laughs again. "I myself do not know how to read or write. Not even my name." He opens his arms wide. "Life is what will bring you wisdom," he says, "if you pay attention."

Prof is silent, nodding. Then he looks at me.

"Come on, No. 1," he says. "Try to smile. You have not been alone in failing. Even the chief of police himself cannot stop those car thieves!"

I say nothing. I am not sad about failing. I am sad for Uncle Go-Easy and Emergency and Tuesday and Nike.

"No. 1 has not stopped trying," says Grandfather. "He has not stopped trying to stop those thieves."

I look at Grandfather. He is wrong!

"You had better be wrong," says Grandmother, passing the tree. "Because if that boy tries again, the chief of police himself will not be able to save him from me!"

Prof looks at my face and laughs.

"Come on, No. 1!" he says. "Let us go for a ride in my car!"

"Na-wa-oh!" I jump to my feet. My engine is running, my pistons are going. Prof has overridden my security systems and turned on my ignition.

I run down to the Firebird. The seats are smooth and shiny and clean. Much cleaner than my torn and dirty shorts.

"Don't worry, No. 1!" Prof laughs.

So I jump in.

Now that my engine is going, maybe my brain will think of something to help Uncle Go-Easy and his children.

Something No. 1!
To save my friends!

The No. 1 Car Spotter Is Stolen

I am the No. 1 car spotter in the No. 1 car, driving down the No. 1 road.

There is only one No. 1 car spotter in my whole village. Only one Pontiac Firebird in my whole country, Nigeria. And there is only one road like this in the whole of Africa.

This road goes to the capital city of Lagos in this my country, Nigeria. It goes through many big-big towns. It passes uncountable villages.

Last time I rode in the Firebird, we went to the nearest town. This time Prof drives in the other direction.

"How about it, No. 1?" he says. "Do you want to see the city?"

I leap up so high in my seat that my head hits the roof. I have never seen the city!

Prof laughs. And he puts his foot down.

But I have heard many-many stories about it. In the city people wear fine-fine clothes every

day. Every shop and chop-house has lights that flash and dazzle all night. Cars drive up and down, up and down.

And now I am here. In the city! For the very first time! I twist about in my seat with my eyes popping from my head. Everything I have heard, it is all true!

"Let us stop here to buy pizza," Prof says, "before your neck twists off your body."

Prof parks outside a chop-house with a red flashing sign. PIZZA HUT.

He looks at my torn and dirty shorts. Prof sighs and I know why.

In the village my clothes are exactly what is required for collecting firewood and herding goats. My fine-fine clothes are stored in the bottom box in my mother's room. They are only for weddings and parties. But here in the city, I can see already that my clothes make me look like a beggar boy. I cannot enter Pizza Hut like this.

"Wait here, No. 1," Prof says. "I will go and get us pizza. We can eat in the car."

"OK, sa'!" I say. Nothing can make me sad today. I am in the city!

"And watch my car for me," Prof says. "Don't let those car thieves take it."

"OK, sa'!" I laugh. "Yes, sa'!"

When Prof has gone into Pizza Hut I jump into the back of the car. There is a new Esclade parked behind us I want to see.

When I jump on the back seat I knock Prof's briefcase onto the floor. It opens and papers spill under the seats. What will Prof say? I squeeze onto the floor to reach the papers. Then the driver's door opens. Prof is back already!

Then the passenger door opens as well. Before I can move, a voice speaks.

"Drive'am, drive'am!"

"Hurry, hurry!" says the voice from the passenger seat again.

"Don' hassle me, man," says the driver. "You think I no sabi drive?"

But that is not Prof's voice. Neither of them is Prof's voice. There are two men in the car and neither of them is Prof. I am on the floor, my body stiff like firewood. The Firebird zooms off.

I open my mouth to shout. "Be quiet, No. 1," orders my brain. "You saw what these people did to Sissy and Uncle Go-Easy." My mouth closes.

"Tonight," says the first man, "we escape with all the cars. The ship is ready. This is the last car we steal. Nobody can catch us now!" He laughs.

Then I remember Grandfather saying, "No. 1 has not finished trying. He has not finished trying to catch those car thieves."

But it is not true. I have not caught the car thieves. It is they who have caught me.

"Do you not think the police are watching the harbour?" the driver asks.

"Many ships will be loading cars tonight," answers the first voice. "Nobody will know ours are stolen. Anyway," he says with a laugh, "we will take the chief of police a message. To make him look the other way."

"Wha' kin' of message?" the driver asks.

"That the stolen cars are leaving the country tonight," the first man replies. "In convoy across the desert!"

The thieves laugh. The car drives for a long time. I am shaking with fear. Will they load me onto a ship too? Will I ever see Mama and Sissy and Grandfather again? Suddenly I hear creaking and groaning, like the sound of our old wooden village cart, but louder.

The car slows. We drive into a dark and quiet place. The Firebird stops.

"This is the last car," the driver says. "And it is a good one. When we sell all of these cars overseas we will be rich. Rich!"

"O-ya," says the passenger. "Let us eat before we take the chief his message."

The two men jump out. They slam the doors. I hear their footsteps walk away. My brain goes into gear.

"O-ya, le's go," it says. "Unless you want to be loaded onto that ship tonight!"

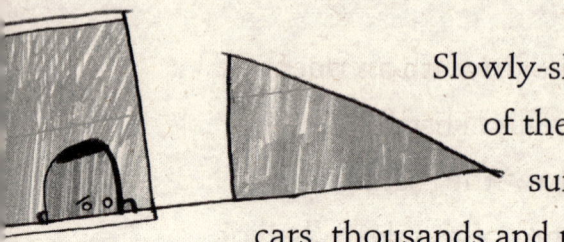

Slowly-slowly, I look out of the window. I am surrounded by cars, thousands and millions of cars. In a building with no windows. I can see nobody. I can hear nobody. I want to get back to my village – even if I have to run all the way. I have had enough of city life!

My hand pulls the door handle. The door opens silently. I crawl out of the Firebird. My body is so stiff, so paining. I crawl between the cars. Yellow Porsche 911, black BMW X-5, red Mercedes ML 320.

I pass behind an SUV with an open door. Suddenly I hear voices. The thieves' voices!

"HIDE NOW!" my brain screams.

I jump in and climb through to the back of the SUV. I roll into a ball. The thieves get in. I am trapped again, with the thieves.

"Le's go! Le's go!" says one.

We drive out into the city. The car thieves have stolen me again! How am I supposed to catch them if they keep catching me?

Today I have been inside more cars than I have ever been in my life. But each time I have been shaking on the floor. This is not a No. 1 situation. "But you are the No. 1," my brain speaks up. "You have spotted the car thieves but they have not spotted you!"

The SUV stops but the engine is still running. The passenger is speaking to somebody.

"We have information for the chief," he says. "Confidential."

"Enter, enter!" a voice shouts.

Slowly we drive on. And park.

"When we have delivered our message," growls the passenger, "we will return to wait with the cars until we load them on the ship tonight!"

"And tomorrow we will be rich!" The driver laughs.

They get out, slamming the doors behind them.

I can hear car engines, reversing, parking, starting up and quenching. I can hear voices. But none of them near the SUV. Carefully I look out.

I am in a yard full of police officers and police cars! This must be the city police station. Why have the thieves brought me here?

Then I remember what they said: "A message for the chief of police! To make him look the other way!"

The thieves have come here to trick the chief of police! To tell him that the cars will leave the country across the desert. Then he will not look towards the ships!

I must warn him. I must find the chief of police and warn him now! Then the thieves will be caught. The Firebird will not be lost. The chief will return me to my mother. The rich will come back and eat in Mama Coca-Cola's chop-house again. And Coca-Cola will go to school!

I jump out of the
SUV into the police yard.
Three big police cars, sirens
blasting, come screeching in front of me.
There is no time to run. There is no time to
hide. The cars stop.

A police officer jumps out of the front
of the biggest car. He opens the back door.
A small man in uniform gets out. He looks
at me.

"Since when were beggar boys allowed in my police yard?" he asks.

The police officer pushes me towards the gate.

"Commot! Go!" he says. "Did you not hear the chief?"

The chief? The small man is the chief of police! I need to speak to him! I dodge the police officer's arms. But the chief is disappearing into the police station. He is gone.

The police officer drags me to the gates.

Outside those gates, along with all the fine-fine people, are all the beggars in the world. Outside those gates the buildings reach to the sky and people sleep underneath rotting cardboard. A city like this can devour a small boy like me.

"Psss!"

The police officer turns around. It is the driver of the police chief's car who is calling.

"Make the beggar boy come wash the chief's cars!" he shouts.

The police officer lets go of me. I run back to the cars. I have escaped the teeth of the city. And maybe now I will see the chief again.

"Wash these cars," the driver says, "and I will give you money for akara."

Happily I take the bucket and cloth. The driver crawls onto the back seat of one of the cars to sleep.

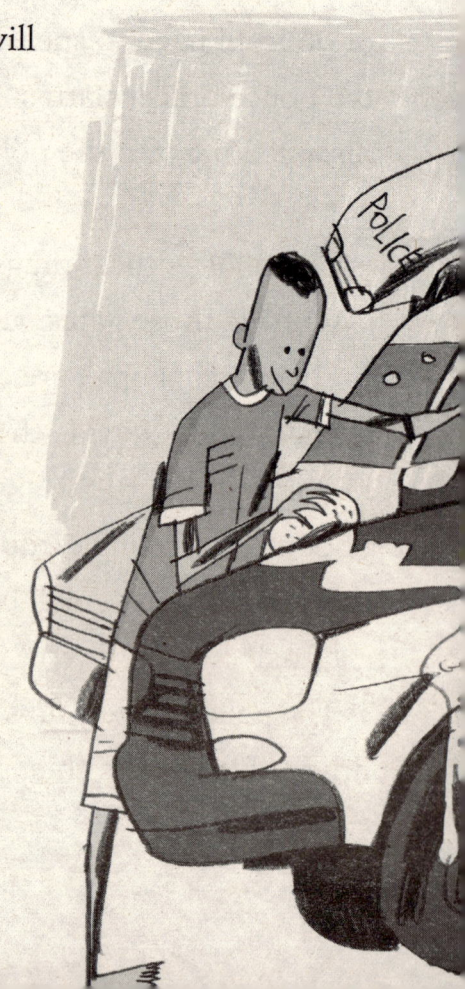

Slowly I begin to wash the cars. Soon the chief of police will come out of his office. And I will still be here. Those thieves will tell him one thing but I will tell him another.

He will catch the thieves and I will catch a bus back to my village!

The No. 1 Car Spotter Spots the Car Thieves

I am the No. 1 car spotter. Pretending to be a No. 1 beggar boy washing the chief of police's cars.

The driver sleeps in the back seat while I wash and polish. Polish and wash. After a while the door at the top of the police station bangs open. Policemen all around the yard salute.

The police chief's driver leaps out of the car and jumps to attention as well.

Out of the police station steps the chief of police. And the car thieves are with him!

They are smiling and shaking hands with him! He is smiling too!

I am so afraid.

I jump inside the back of the car where the driver was sleeping. I crouch on the floor. I hear the thieves' SUV drive away.

The chief of police is speaking. "Police officers, get into your cars," he says. "Tonight we apprehend the car thieves."

"Where, sir?" a policeman asks.

"That is confidential information," says the chief. "You will follow my car."

"Urgent telephone call, sir!" I hear somebody shout.

Two police officers jump into the front of the escort car. I crouch down lower. They don't see me.

"I have never seen the chief vex like this," one of them says.

"It is those car thieves," says the other, and he sucks his teeth. "People are saying the chief of police cannot stop them. Not even if they took his own car."

"If I find those thieves," says the first, "I will bang their heads together."

"No need." The other laughs. "You are a police officer. You can simply handcuff them and throw them into jail."

Both policemen laugh.

"I can find them for you!" somebody shouts.

Before I realize that it was me that shouted, there are two policemen looking down at me.

My brain puts its head in its hands.

The policemen look at me. I look at them.

"It is that beggar boy," says one of them to the other. "What are you doing in my police car?" he says to me.

"I know where the thieves are hiding the stolen cars," I say.

The police officers laugh loudly.

"And since when did we fraternize with beggar boys in my car?" shouts a loud voice.

All of us jump. It is the chief of police, come back out of the police station.

The police officers jump out of the car and salute. I copy them.

"What is going on here!" shouts the chief.

Speak now! says my brain. But my mouth is opening and closing like a fish's.

"We found this boy hiding in the back of the car," says one of the policemen.

The police chief looks at me. "As if I do not have enough on my hands!" he shouts. "Take him away."

The policemen take hold of me.

My mouth retrieves my voice from my stomach.

"The car thieves are trying to trick you!" I croak. "They are escaping by ship tonight!"

But the chief of police is walking away. And he does not stop.

"They will take all those fine-fine cars out of our country!" I am shouting now. "Even our one and only Pontiac Firebird!"

The chief of police stops. He stands still. He turns back around to face me.

"What did you say?" he asks.

"They took Prof's car," I say. "He asked me to watch it. But I was too afraid to stop them."

"Chief, don't waste your time," says one of the policemen.

"Wait!" says the chief. "I had a call from Prof just now. He said his Firebird had been stolen. With a village boy inside!"

"This boy is probably working with the thieves," says the police officer.

I look at him.

"I am the No. 1 car spotter," I say. "The No. 1 car spotter in my village. I am NOT a car thief."

The chief of police smiles.

"That is exactly what Prof said," he says. "So you made your way to the police station to report the theft. You are a brave boy."

I shake my head.

"I am not brave," I said. "I was carried to the station in the back of the car thieves' car."

"What?" shouts the chief.

I tell the chief of police how I hid in the back of the Firebird and then in the back of the SUV.

"Those men who came to give you information," I say, "they are the car thieves."

"They are private detectives," the chief of police explains to me. "Working for a lady who has had more than five cars stolen."

"They are not detectives!" I shout. "They are car thieves!"

The chief sighs.

"No. 1," he says. "Either I believe two grown men or I believe one small boy. I cannot be in two places at once tonight. The police force is already stretched thin."

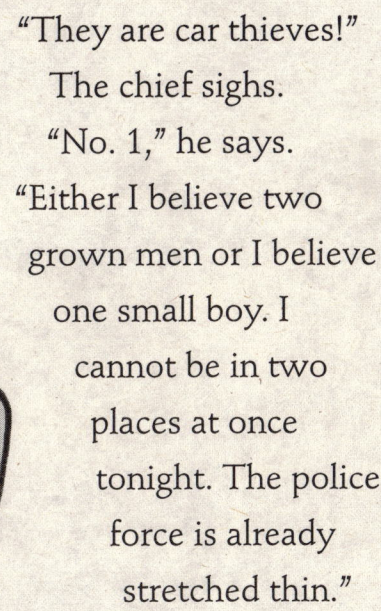

"Sir," says a police officer. "How can what he says be true? How could he have been hiding on the floor of all those cars without being noticed?"

"I was on the floor of your car." I eye him. "I heard you say that you would bang the heads of the thieves together."

The chief laughs. Then he sighs.

"I cannot go to the harbour because a small boy tells me to."

He pats my head.

And walks away.

"They are not going through the desert!"
I shout. "They are trying to trick you!"

The chief stops again. His back is stiff.

"What did you say?" he asks.

"The thieves are trying to trick you."
I am crying now. "They want you to go to
the desert so you do not see them escape
by ship."

The police officers look at each other.

"How do you know they told me to go
to the desert?" The chief looks at me hard.
"This is confidential information."

"I was hiding on the floor of the SUV
listening." I sob. "I heard them say they
were going to tell you about a
convoy across the desert so
that you would be far from
the harbour."

The chief of police takes
out his phone.

"Prof," I hear him say. "I have your No. 1 boy here."

"No. 1? Thank God!" I hear Prof say. Then I hear him shout, "They have found him! The police have found him!"

"Prof, I do not know whether I can trust his story," the chief says.

"You can trust him one hundred percent," says Prof. "He is a No. 1 boy."

The chief closes his phone and looks at me.

"He is a beggar boy," says one of the police officers. "Look at him."

"I am a village boy," I say. "I herd goats and carry firewood. I would be a foolish boy to do that in fine-fine clothes."

The chief smiles.

"Even if he was a beggar boy," he says to the police officer, "would that mean he did not have a brain?"

"A No. 1 brain!" I say.

"OK, No. 1." The chief of police laughs. "Tell me everything!"

So I tell the chief the whole story from the beginning. I even tell him how I think the thieves used their laptops to override the cars' security systems.

"Na-wa-oh!" the police officers gasp.

"You see," the chief of police tells them. "A No. 1 brain can take any disguise." Then he says, "Let us change our clothes. Night has come and we have thieves to catch."

It is true. As we have been talking, night has come. The stolen cars will be loading onto the ship any minute now!

The chief and police officers go inside. They leave me sitting outside. Somebody brings me akara and Coca-Cola! When the police come out I do not recognize them! Their uniforms are gone. They are wearing the clothes of labourers, old and torn. Their skin is dirty, their eyes are red.

"No. 1, we have copied your disguise." The smallest man winks.

We all follow him out of the side door of the compound. As we walk along the road the stink of the roadside gutter is strong in my nose. A mammy-wagon passes us. There are many men in the back with rough voices and dirty faces. When the wagon slows, the chief and his officers jump into the back. I run and they pull me up too. Nobody looks at us.

I squat in the back of the bumping, bouncing lorry, holding on to the side. I keep my mouth shut.

When I hear creaking and groaning
I stand up. We are in a yard of big ships.
It is ships making this creaking and
groaning! Big lights show that cars are
being driven out of big-big buildings and
onto each ship.

But they cannot *all* be stolen cars!
Which ship is being loaded with the
stolen cars?

The mammy-wagon slows.
Nobody looks at us. We are only
a broken lorry full of men who
have come to work and sweat.

The chief squats on the floor next to me. He looks into my eyes.

"We cannot make a mistake now," he says. "You are the No. 1 car spotter. Spot those stolen cars!"

I stand up. I do not look at the ships. I do not look at the buildings. I do not look at the men. I look at the cars.

Daewoos, Mercedes Benz, BMWs, Range Rovers, Lamborghinis, Nissans. There are so many-many cars. Then I spot a yellow Porsche 911, a black BMW X-5, a red Mercedes ML 320!

Those were the cars I saw in the building. The stolen cars!

The chief leans his ear to my mouth.

"Big orange ship," I whisper. "Longest line. I have seen those cars before."

The chief hesitates. "Are you sure?"

I am not sure! There may be many-many yellow Porsche 911s, black BMW X-5s, red Mercedes ML 320s in the shipyard.

Carefully I scan each line of cars entering the orange ship. I spot each car. Then I see it!

The Firebird! The red Pontiac Firebird!

"There is only one Firebird in this country!" I point.

The chief and his men leap from the mammy-wagon. They scatter behind the buildings and run crouching along the lines of cars ... and catch the car thieves!

"HANDS UP!" they shout.

* * *

Now it is morning. All night the police have been busy rounding up car thieves.

"Let's have breakfast," says the chief.

"Pizza Hut?" I ask.

The chief laughs and slaps my back. "Anything you say, No. 1."

We collect the pizza in the car of the chief of police. And now I cannot wait to see Mama and Sissy. I cannot wait to tell Grandfather and Coca-Cola everything.

Maybe even Grandmother will have forgiven me by now.

She definitely will when she sees what I have in my pocket. An envelope with reward money. A reward big enough to pay for Uncle Go-Easy's hospital bills!

In the village everybody is waiting. Even Uncle Go-Easy!

Their eyes pop out of their heads when they see me arrive with the chief of police himself.

The chief shakes hands with Grandfather.

"I hear you trained this boy yourself," he says.

"It was a small thing," says Grandfather.

"A small thing?" says the chief. "From now on car spotting is of No. 1 national importance! And this is our No. 1 boy!"

Everybody cheers. They throw me in the air like I scored a World Cup goal.

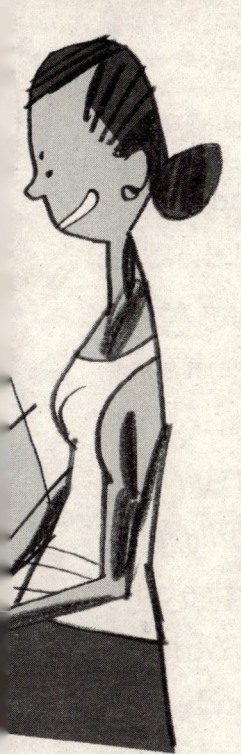

I am the No. 1. The No. 1 car spotter. Not just in my own village, but in my whole entire country – maybe in the whole entire world.

I can spot a car fast enough to catch a thief!

Atinuke was born in Nigeria and spent her childhood in both Africa and the UK. She is the author of the bestselling Anna Hibiscus and No. 1 Car Spotter series set in contemporary Nigeria, as well as award winning non-fiction books *Africa, Amazing Africa: Country by Country* and *Brilliant Black British History*. Atinuke is also an oral storyteller of tales from the African continent and diaspora. She currently lives on a mountain overlooking the sea in West Wales. Visit her website at atinuke.co.uk

Warwick Johnson Cadwell lives by the Sussex seaside with his smashing family and pets. Most of his time is spent drawing, or thinking about drawing, but for a change of scenery he also skippers boats. The *No. 1 Car Spotter Fights the Factory* is his eighth book for Walker Books.